# Maybe Connie Was Only Grateful To Him, Tweed Thought.

Maybe she didn't actually care about him. What if she was only clinging to him because he had saved her and he was protective of her?

He lay in the dark with that dear woman in his arms, against his hot body, and he wondered if when she healed she would be strong enough to leave him.

How could he be sure that she didn't cling to him just because she'd been so terrified, and he was somebody to hold so that she could feel safe?

He considered that soberly as he stared into the night. He knew he couldn't give her up. How could he bind her to him so tightly that she wouldn't think of leaving him?

Dear Reader,

As the weather gets cold, cold, cold, Silhouette Desire gets hot, hot, hot! (If you live in Florida, Southern California or some other *warm* place, just imagine us living up north, *freezing!*) Anyway, here at Desire, we're generating *our* heat from six sensuous stories written by six spectacular authors. And they're all here, this month, in our HEAT UP YOUR WINTER collection.

Just take a look at this fabulous line-up: a *Man of the Month* from Lass Small; the next installment in the SOMETHING WILD series by Ann Major; and fantastic stories by Dixie Browning, Barbara Boswell, Mary Lynn Baxter and Robin Elliott. And I'm sure you've already noticed that this is one of our now-famous MONTHS OF MEN, with six sinfully sexy hero portraits on the front covers. (Aren't these guys *cute?*)

At Silhouette Desire we're dedicated to bringing you the very best short, sexy books around. Let us know—do you think we're succeeding? Are the books *too* sexy? Could you stand some more sizzle? Or maybe you think they're "just right." Write me! I'm here to listen.

In the meantime, HEAT UP YOUR WINTER with Silhouette Desire.

All the best,

Lucia Macro
Senior Editor

# LASS SMALL
## TWEED

SILHOUETTE *Desire*

Published by Silhouette Books

America's Publisher of Contemporary Romance

SILHOUETTE BOOKS

ISBN 0-373-05817-9

TWEED

**Books by Lass Small**

Silhouette Desire

*Tangled Web #241*
*To Meet Again #322*
*Stolen Day #341*
*Possibles #356*
*Intrusive Man #373*
*To Love Again #397*
*Blindman's Bluff #413*

*Goldilocks and the Behr #437
*Hide and Seek #453
*Red Rover #491
*Odd Man Out #505
*Tagged #534
*Contact #548*
*Wrong Address, Right Place #569*
*Not Easy #578*
*The Loner #594*
*Four Dollars and Fifty-One Cents #613*
*No Trespassing Allowed #638
*The Molly Q #655*
†*'Twas the Night #684*
*Dominic #697
†*A Restless Man #731*
†*Two Halves #743*
†*Beware of Widows #755*
*A Disruptive Influence #775*
†*Balanced #800*
†*Tweed #817*

*Lambert Series
†Fabulous Brown Brothers

Silhouette Romance

*An Irritating Man #444*
*Snow Bird #521*

Silhouette Books

*Silhouette Christmas Stories* 1989
"Voice of the Turtles"

*Silhouette Spring Fancy* 1993
"Chance Encounter"

---

## LASS SMALL

finds living on this planet at this time a fascinating experience. People are amazing. She thinks that to be a teller of tales of people, places and things is absolutely marvelous.

To my daughter
Liza
who minds my p's and q's

with my love

# One

___

Out in West Texas, flying a Piper Cub, Tweed Brown was spending a perfect, beautiful day looking for a brush bull. The bull was one of the smart ones. He was a renegade that could fade from sight, perfectly. And by then he had stolen at least five cows to start his own harem. Finding him before he cownapped any more would be tough going. Damned greedy bull.

Five cows were enough for any bull.

But Tweed thought how it might be for a man to have five women. A tall, long-legged one. Yeah. One who was short and cuddly, one shy, a bold one...yep. He smiled. And one who was plump and giggly. A choice group.

Tweed became a little moony, and his searching glance around was somewhat more tolerant.

Then he remembered reading that a woman needed five men as husbands! A guy who could repair anything, a social type that was polite and could dance, one that liked kids and monitored them, a workaholic to make the living to support the whole bunch... and a lover.

How like a woman to be selfish and want it all.

Tweed frowned and thought maybe he ought to skip searching for the bull. In this world, there ought to be one male that could have things his way, even if it was only a bull. He was at least trying for the good life.

The ground wind wasn't quite so brisk, and it was a great September day. Tweed spoke into the little wire curl on his headphone, giving his direction and gas supply. He added, "Everything looks okay. And old Hugo is nowhere around."

While Tweed was actually talking to himself, the transmission was being recorded on tape back at the house. Today it was Jimmy who would check the tape each hour.

In the little plane, Tweed buzzed along like a large, lazy insect. Lifting in order to clear the next hill, he came over the top of the rise and his view could then include the next hollow.

There was a smudge of smoke.

It wasn't a brushfire. Someone was burning something? He lifted a bit higher to be out of rifle-shot range. A man never knew what he might find in the brush. Tweed became very alert.

Talking into the wire, he gave an account of what was going on. "Smoke. Not a brushfire. There's a tire?" He confirmed it. "Somebody's burning a tire!"

That was the classic SOS in the wide, peopleless stretches of the West. A traveler carried an extra tire and a bottle of flammable oil to ignite it. Anyone seeing the resulting smoke would know something was wrong. The black smoke called for attention just like circling buzzards did. To get attention, burning a tire was better than waiting for buzzards.

Tweed said to the wire, "Uh. There's a car. I don't see a soul. The tire's about spent. That's been burning a long, long time. The ground wind dissipated it as it rose from this hollow. Bad place to get caught. Wonder why he didn't carry the tire to the rim of the hill?"

Tweed circled closer, lower, watching. "He might be hurt. Car looks okay. A very dusty pale blue station wagon. I'd say about a '78 Ford. It's partly under a mesquite, but it apparently didn't hit the tree."

He circled again, watching to see if anyone came out to signal, but no one did. Tweed frowned.

"Looks spooky. It could be a trap. But maybe somebody's in real trouble. If I don't call in pronto, come a-humping. I'm going to land and look around."

Being extremely careful, he flew the tiny plane along just above the rocky track, watching to see if he could land on it. It was marginally plausible.

What if there was more than one person? His tiny plane couldn't hold more than two people. A pilot and somebody else.

He pulled the plane up, circled and went back, slowing almost to a stall and landing carefully. He jounced along and finally jolted to a stop. They just might have to bring some of the guys or a cow pony from the ranch to pull the plane out of there. A real cow pony knew what to do with something that didn't want to move.

Great, he thought sourly. If the person was badly hurt, or if he couldn't get the plane out of there,

there'd be two of them trapped. They could then light another tire. He sucked his tongue against his teeth once in a disgusted way.

Well, whoever lit that tire was a human, and any human was worth the effort. And any human who sent up such a signal needed help. He had it. Tweed Brown was there.

He shut off the engine. The plane's noise had silenced the creatures in the hollow. In the stillness, Tweed considered his isolation. No one called out. What if the person was already rescued? No. They'd have put out the tire fire.

He told the wire, "I've landed. Stick around when you get back."

He took off the headphone and got out of the little plane.

He was a plain-looking man and stood tall, just over six feet. His hair was dark, his eyes blue. He was built like a man who worked hard and enjoyed the work. His shirt and trousers were denim. The sleeves were long and the cuffs buttoned.

He wore gloves that were made for his hands, protecting them while giving him the freedom of doing what needed to be done. His feet were protected by worn boots that had been made specifically for him.

He was just past thirty. Physical exertion had formed him into a beautifully made male.

He reached back into the plane, took out and buckled on a gun belt, settling it on his hips. He looked around in the dead silence as he put the Stetson on his head. He was ready for...whatever.

Down in that hollow, there was no sound. No breeze. Like everywhere else, the trees were mostly mesquite but there was an oak or so. Some cottonwoods were across the way where there was probably moisture. A seep?

The weeds were brittle and high where there was soil. The ground was mostly rock slabs with dirt gathered in the rock folds.

He shouted, "Hallooo!"

There was only the silence.

He took the first-aid kit from the holder and turned toward the smudge to watch it, narrow eyed. He looked around, turning his head and listening.

Anyone who'd been there, presumably the person who had lit that tire, would have heard the plane; and if he could, he would have called out—unless he was dead.

Or... if it was a trap. Somebody wanted the plane? That had happened to their neighbor a couple of years back. Smugglers who'd gotten away from the law and done this very thing. Old Kenny had flown out and got himself killed. Somehow the bastards had gotten Kenny into the plane with them. He'd been shoved out of the plane. The only way the searchers had found him was because the buzzards had led them to the body.

The plane's ignition key was in Tweed's pocket. The key had a magnet on it. He moved around, lifting the tail of the plane around so it was heading outward to leave that place. He put a stone under both sides of one wheel, fiddling around, and placed the key quite cleverly.

He moved cautiously, pausing, listening, turning his head, watching. He had an odd feeling that wasn't fear. It was... excitement.

Why?

And he thought, by God, what if he ran into Hugo and his harem right there in that hollow? On foot. Now wouldn't that be cute! He didn't think Hugo would be too friendly. He was really a brush bull.

What they should do, Tweed had argued, was leave the renegade out there, supply him with cows and let him breed them all. His cows dropped superior beef.

So Tweed was looking for a victim, then for smugglers, and on top of that, for a hostile bull...just about in that order.

"Halllooooo!" he called again.

And he saw the person. It silently stepped into view. It wasn't a man, so it had to be a woman. She had on an old, wide-brimmed, floppy hat that was too big for her, and a long, shapeless denim jacket that went down to her knees and was equally loose.

She had a rifle. It was pointed at him. She said, "Take off the gun belt and throw it over here."

Hell. "Are you the burned tire, or are you freelancing?"

"Do as I said."

"Why don't I just go back to my plane and leave you alone here?"

"Take off the gun belt and throw it over here."

"You've said that. I don't want to. I'm ticked."

"Do it."

He watched as she lifted the rifle and aimed it at his heart...exactly.

Tweed's foster father Salty Brown of Temple, Ohio, had told Tweed specifically that nobody ever argues with a rifle. So faced with such a situation, Tweed muttered really nasty curses as he undid the belt and held it. He took a deep breath and said, "You're a good argument not to stop off and help anyone."

"Do it. Throw it over here."

He did that.

She picked it up quite easily and put it very naturally over her shoulder. She looked like a *bandito*. The gun was carried with knowledgeable skill and was now pointed to the ground, but it was ready. He respected that she could do whatever she wanted with that gun.

"If you want cash, I don't carry it on me. I'm not worth anything held for ransom. That's not my plane."

"Turn around."

Instead, he squatted down and pulled on the tab that produced a bag of tobacco from his shirt pocket. He proceeded to carefully roll a cigarette.

He was madder than a wet hen or a newly castrated calf, but he saw that his hands were perfectly steady. That was something for a man in those circumstances. He was peripherally amused.

With some snide push, he asked, "You have other rescuers around?"

"I suppose you could have called them that."

That stopped him. He looked up at her, frowning, seeing her more clearly. He asked slowly, "Are you all right?"

"Now."

Then he could see under the brim of that oversize hat that there were the reddened marks of new bruises on her face.

He started to rise, but the gun came back on him. Softly he asked, "My God, woman, what happened?"

"I was...rescued."

"Who?"

"No one I knew."

Knew? Past tense? "Tell me." His voice was somewhat stern.

"I see no reason to entertain you."

"Are they dead?"

"Yes."

He slowly stood up. Unthreatening, he looked around, alert, coiled. "None got away?"

"No."

"How many were there?"

"Two."

He looked at her intently. "Can you fly a plane?"

"No."

"Let me get you to a hospital."

"How can I know you—"

"On my word. My name's Tweed Brown. I work for Sam Fuller. His land lies along this area to the north. I'm looking for a rogue bull."

"I found two."

He was standing, his hands to his sides. His unlit cigarette was now abandoned on the ground. He told her earnestly, "I swear to you that you're safe with me. Let me put the signal fire out. Is there something I can do for your car? Can it be fixed? Why are you here, in this place? Alone?"

"I wasn't."

"Someone was with you?"

"Yes."

"And?"

"He, too, is dead."

"Aw. This is terrible for you. Come. Let me fly you to the hospital. We can get help for you. I'll put out the fire and see to the people. Which was the one with you? Let me cover him so he won't be—"

"He's in the car. He . . . his . . . body is safe."

"You're in shock. We need to get you back to people. You need some care. Can you trust me?"

"That's about what they said."

"Let me be sure they're dead."

"I made sure."

"You know my name." His voice was gentle but firm. "I need to know yours."

"No."

"I have to look at them. I have to check them out. You must realize that. Go to the plane and get inside. I'll be back."

Expecting anything to happen, he slowly turned and carefully walked off to the side. He was braced to be shot. It wouldn't have surprised him. But he thought she would warn him first. She hadn't shot him when he landed. She could have.

He went and put out the fire. They didn't need to attract anyone else. Then he saw that it had been extinguished once before, and she'd relit it. It must have taken great desperation for her to do that.

He went to the car and found the hood up. There were tools out.

He found the bodies. He saw the marks of the struggle. He saw her marks on the men. They had been shot. Somebody had used a knife on them. The blood was darkened. The bodies were stiffened, and the smell of death was there.

The man in the car was older. Her father? He was badly beaten. It had to have been horrific for a man to be killed with a beating like that. It stirred a feeling of revenge in Tweed that shook him.

Or had his urge for revenge been caused by the trap, now past, that the woman had survived? His emotions were such that he could not think of what the woman had endured. But he wondered how she'd managed.

He knew the incident had never been intended as anything else. They had extinguished the fire.

She and the older man would have been left there forever. Dragged off by animals, their bones might have never been found.

And again, Tweed thought of what it had cost her to relight that tire.

Having to use some effort with the awkwardly stiffened bodies, he dumped them into the back seat and closed the car doors. Then he returned to her.

She had her back to him, frozen. She was in shock. Moving carefully, keeping about fifteen feet away, he went around her and to the plane. He retrieved the key and took it to her, opening his palm and holding the key out to her.

From under the brim of that big, tacky straw hat, she looked at the key.

Tweed said, "This is the key to the plane."

"All right."

He took her response to mean that she would go with him. He went back to the plane and opened the door. He turned and watched her. She came slowly, as if she was walking against a strong current. She stopped and looked back for some time.

Tweed told her, "Some of the boys and I will come back with the sheriff."

"Yes."

Understanding that she was in shock, his words were careful. "If you will sit here, I'll show you how to do the harness."

"I know."

"Will you kindly put the guns in the back? Just behind the seat. You can put the rifle flat with the barrel pointed across the plane and put my gun down on the floor just behind you. See? There's room enough. Please empty the rifle. I'd hate a surprise discharge."

She emptied the chamber. She hadn't touched his handgun. She put them as he'd instructed, her back to him. She trusted him. Maybe she was in such shock that she couldn't not trust someone.

He kicked away the rocks by the wheel. She didn't say anything. He got her inside and into the harness. Her hand was like ice.

He removed his Stetson, got into the plane and put on the radio headgear. He saw that it was past the hour, and Jimmy would be there. He called in to the ranch. "Stand by. Jimmy, I'm trying to get out of here. I have a lady who is in shock. I'll fly over to the hospital. Will you call ahead and have someone standing by there?"

"Got it. Roger. What's going on?"

"Get the sheriff and go to the area I gave you. The older man was with this lady."

"Who is it?"

So that they could be warned, Tweed corrected gently: "Was." Then he added carefully, "I don't know."

The takeoff was an experience he wasn't anxious to repeat. They did make it, missed the crucial tree and lifted over the hill. He flew her to the hospital.

On the ground below, Tweed recognized that Sanford was the doctor waiting. He wasn't much older than Tweed, and they were good friends. Tweed landed perfectly in the chancy crosswind, turned the plane and taxied back to the entrance. Two orderlies were there with a cart.

Next to him, the woman stiffened in a jerk and shivered. The need to be functional was passing, and she was going deeper into shock? In a carefully soothing voice, he said, "I'll go with you. These are good men. They're people I know. They won't hurt you." He made the words slow and careful.

The plane stopped. One orderly put blocks under the wheels.

Sanford opened the plane door as the propeller whispered its last cycles. "What's up?" He was looking at the woman, and he saw her. He understood... that quickly. He said, "Yes." He told the orderlies, "We need to wrap her, she's going into shock." He said to Tweed, "Come with us. Give your key to Pete."

Then Sanford called, "Pete! Come move this plane to the parking area. Please."

From some distance was the reply, "Yes, sir."

They put her on the cart and wrapped her. Then they trundled her to the entrance. As they went, Sanford asked Tweed, "Is she bleeding?"

"I don't know."

"What happened?"

Under the sound of the rolling cart wheels, Tweed replied softly just for Sanford's hearing, "It was a burning tire I investigated. Assault. Two men."

"Damn."

Tweed took Sanford's arm and allowed the cart to go ahead a little as he added, "They killed the man with her. They beat him to death."

"My God."

"Yes."

Sanford asked, "What's her name?"

"I don't know."

"Give what information you can to Polly at the desk. We've got to work with her. Stick around."

"All right."

Sanford said, "It could be a while."

"I'll be talking to Betty Lou."

"You leave Betty Lou alone."

Tweed asked, "Oh?"

But Sanford's steps had stretched out and he was gone.

So having been warned to stay away from Betty Lou, Tweed did go see what she was doing. She smiled and that charming dimple appeared with such magic that a man was forced to find nice things to say so she'd smile again. "How come Sanford told me to leave you alone?"

"I don't know."

"Now don't you go and try to fool this ole boy, you must have some clue he cottons to you."

"When did you ever hear tell of that?"

"He just told me I was to leave you be. How come he said that?"

She shrugged pretty shoulders so her uniform was pulled against her nice, round breasts, and she said, "I don't know." Then she pushed her hair back from her neck and asked, "Why're you here?"

"I found a lady who needed some serious help. Sanford'll tell you about her. I don't know much."

Then Polly came looking for Tweed. "The sheriff called and said for you to stay put, he'll be here as soon as he can. What's going on?"

"I don't know. I just found a lady who needed some very serious help, and I brought her to you all."

Betty Lou said, "We'll take care of her. Is she anyone you know?"

"No."

Polly asked, "What's her name?"

And again Tweed said, "I don't know."

Betty Lou asked, "Is she from around these parts?"

"I have no idea."

The hospital was in the middle of nowhere. It was a
consolidated medical center that was supported by the
several towns and a bunch of ranches that were in that
area. Just the fact that it had a landing strip was an
indication of the range of people who used the place.

It was well equipped. It could handle anything. It
could handle a traumatized woman.

As it turned out, they had a hard time finding out
who the patient was that Tweed had brought in. She
was in shock and unconscious. They allowed that. She
needed the time to heal.

The sheriff told Tweed that the car at the scene,
where Tweed had found the woman, had no registra-
tion. The vehicle identification numbers had been filed
off.

There were fingerprints, but those couldn't be traced
because they weren't on file. One of the men was
probably an alien.

There was speculation that if the woman and the
older man had been brought there against their wishes,
why had there been the signal fire? Or if they had been
caught there unawares, someone else had taken their
car, left them stranded and they'd been surprised by
the two men. In that very isolated place, there were tire
tracks of another car.

So the search began. The sheriff's office sent out inquiries and then waited to hear if anyone was missing. The older man's fingerprints weren't registered. Apparently, neither of the victims of the assault had been in the armed forces, and they had never been in any job that required fingerprinting.

The woman continued in a coma, and the sheriff nagged Tweed. "You're the only one who spoke to her. How did she sound?"

"Brief."

The sheriff gave Tweed a patient glance of irony and sighed. "What exactly did she say?"

"You know everything I heard from her. I can't add anything. You've rattled my brains on this. It's still as I've told you. She spoke like a woman who was educated. She talks like an American. Not necessarily a Texan." He added that thoughtfully. Then he repeated, yet again, "She handled the rifle and the gun belt as if she was familiar with them. She walked with authority. Her voice is pleasant. I can't give you any information on the man. He was already dead."

The sheriff commented, "There's no luggage. No extra clothes. None at all for her. No rings or earrings, no watches. Nothing. They weren't from around here. Nobody has reported such people as missing."

Tweed said needlessly, "The only people who can answer your questions are dead, or close to it."

"I wish..."

When the sheriff didn't finish his sentence, Tweed said, "I know this worries you. But you know all that I know and probably a whole lot more. You'll just have to wait until she wakes up."

"If she does."

"Yeah. But. She struck me as being a strong woman. She'll come around."

However, she continued to avoid waking. Everyone talked to her. She did not respond.

Then the sheriff asked Tweed to go see her. Tweed was a little reluctant. He had reason to know that she'd been badly used, and it hurt him to see anything that had been harmed—unless he could do something about it.

But he did go to the hospital. He wore clean jeans and a plaid cotton shirt. He took a bouquet of flowers. By then it'd been over a week since he'd brought her there. He saw the bruises on her face had darkened. She really looked battered. Seeing her injuries twisted in Tweed's heart.

He sat down by the woman's bed and looked at her. Her breathing was slow. Her body was female under the drawn-up sheet. Her hands were on her stomach. She was so still.

For the strong woman he remembered, she didn't look very strong then. She looked . . . adrift. He took her hand as his glance questioned Sanford if he could do that. Sanford nodded once.

The sheriff whispered, "Ask her."

Tweed frowned at the sheriff before he looked back at the woman. She hadn't been a woman for very long. How old was she? Her blond hair was spread on the pillow. It was clean and . . . kinda soft looking. It tended to wave. There were little curls by her ears and in the little hairs at her temple.

He hadn't known she was blond. Her lashes were a darker blond and lay on her cheeks. The skin around one eye was shadowed by bruises. Her healing lips were soft and still a little swollen on one side, but the cut was healing. It looked like somebody had put a stitch in that one.

He declined to consider how else she might have been harmed.

The sheriff hissed, "Ask her name."

Tweed cleared his throat as he glanced at her immobile face, and he saw that she flinched minutely at the sound.

Sanford's mouth opened in the slightest gasp-sound of indrawn breath. "She heard," Sanford whispered so quietly that it was almost no sound at all.

"Ask her." The sheriff did try for Sanford's whisper, but it was like a steam calliope.

Tweed asked the woman, "How're you today?"

Her lips parted, and she almost frowned.

"What's your name, honey?" His voice was soft, but his compassion made it roughen.

And she wailed, "Ohhhh. Noooo."

It was the most anguished, defeated sound that Tweed had ever heard. But then a tear came from the corner of her eye and that finished him. He scrunched up his eyes and tightened his mouth, but he held her hand as if it were a new chick.

Her breaths were broken.

Tweed stood up and leaned over her. In a very earnest voice, he told her, "I'm Tweed Brown. I rescued you. I brought you to the hospital in a plane. Remember? You're safe now."

With the three men watching intensely, she frowned a little, then her face slowly relaxed, and she . . . went back to wherever she'd been.

But . . . her hand moved in Tweed's and her fingers briefly curled around the edge of his palm.

When Tweed told Sanford she had moved her fingers to hold his palm, the doctor replied, ''It could have been reflex. Come back tomorrow. Let's try it again then. Talk to her.''

Tweed went back to the ranch, and standing on the front porch in the sunset, he told Sam, ''They want me back tomorrow.''

Sam replied, ''Help her. Do what you can.''

Tweed lifted his Stetson and looked far off as he re-settled it. ''Thanks, Sam.'' Then he admitted, ''I was kinda hoping you'd tell me I couldn't go. That there were too many things around here to do.''

Sam smiled and put his fingers backward into the back pockets of his jeans. ''You're a cream puff.''

''You shoulda seen her.''

''I did.''

''Yeah?'' Tweed frowned at his boss. ''When was that?''

''Right away. I had to understand what all you'd had to do. Did you see where they fought?''

''Not really. I was afraid she'd shoot me.''

Sam said, ''We went out right away. To be sure nothing got at the bodies. It was...impressive. That woman must be something.''

Tweed admitted softly, ''She struck me that way. I'm surprised she flipped out.''

Sam explained, ''The brain does that when people can't cope. It gives them some peace until they can heal a little. She'll still have to deal with this, but she can have some time first.''

Tweed studied Sam. ''How do you know all that?''

''I asked.''

# Two

Tweed went back to the hospital the next day, gird-ing his emotions to protect himself a little. How could a man not be compassionate to such a fragile, bat-tered woman? Even the hand he held was bruised.

As Tweed talked to her, Sanford and the sheriff watched avidly for some response.

Sometimes her eyelids would quiver. Once her lips parted and she appeared to try to speak to him. But she did not.

However, when he had taken her slight hand into his big square one, her fingers had curled over the side of his hand with enough pressure that he felt she was holding on to him.

Sanford said, "She'll come around. She'll be all right."

And Tweed remembered the figure coming from

behind the brush to stand on that rocky place, holding the rifle. A pioneer woman facing the savages.

And she had. She had.

In that time, there'd been some articles in the local paper about the unknown young woman who was suffering and unconscious. Tweed Brown was named as her rescuer. The article was picked up by other Texas papers, and some of the newspapers from other states took up the story and reprinted it.

It was a while after the rescue of the unknown woman that Tweed and Sam were having a perfect breakfast. They were complaining to Jake about his lousy cooking when Salty called from Temple, Ohio. Sam handed Tweed the phone, and Salty said, "So that's where you are."

Tweed replied, "You got the voice of this century."

"I've missed you."

"You got the coat?"

"Yep."

" 'Yep'? You musta spent some time in TEXAS."

"You forget my old shipmate, Pepper, over in San Antonio?"

"God, Salty, I coulda used you a while back."

"You need me?"

"I can handle it now."

"What've you got to handle?" Salty's voice had slowed.

Tweed told Salty about finding the woman in the hollow, down south of the ranch, and the circumstances. He added, "She's still unconscious."

"That poor woman." The rasp was gentle.

"When I found her, she was still running on the taggle end of adrenaline and nerves."

"She used up her reserve."

"Yeah."

"What a tough time for the lady. Keep us up on her progress . . . and yours. Felicia wants to talk to you." His voice faded as he said, "Don't be too long."

Tweed didn't know if Salty was talking to Felicia or to him.

In her marvelous stage voice, gentled for him, Felicia said, "Hello, darling. Salty meant you. Don't be too long in calling or writing. We think of you so often, and the kids all ask after you. Are you all right?"

"Yeah. Everything's fine. I'd have called, but I've never had nothing to report about."

"We like to hear your voice. We need to know about you. If it's inconvenient to call, you can always make it collect."

"Yeah. I'll be in touch. How's . . . all the kids?"

Felicia realized Tweed had altered the question from asking about one person to including the whole group. She wondered . . . which one. "Do you know . . . of course, you don't know. We've had a rash of marriages recently. Georgia hooked a man from Indianapolis, Bob is married to Jo Malone, do you remember her?"

"The redhead! Lucky man!"

"He agrees. Then, let's see, who came next? Oh, Cray went down to check on Susanne in San Antonio and couldn't control her, so he married her. Then Mike married a schoolteacher in Indiana—her class had written Mike when he was in the Persian Gulf."

"I wondered if Mike went."

"Yes. He's okay. He's carrying some shrapnel, but so far all is well with him. He's in Texas finishing up his last year with the army. And over in Fort Wayne, Indiana, Rod married the widow next door."

"What happened to Rod's wife? She was a little—different."

"She died. Sat in her chair for two days, dead. She never talked, and the TV was always on. Rod thought she was all right."

"My God."

"It really shook Rod. But you should see his new wife. They have a little girl who is an angel. Then Mitchell went over to Indiana. I know you remember him, Mitchell Goalong. He was here when you lived with us."

"Yeah. What's he doing?"

"He's working for Jamisons, a big store in Fort Wayne, as vice president of marketing."

"Looks like Indiana's been lucky for the Browns. Did you say that Mike and Cray are both in Texas?"

"Yes. So are John and Tom! Give me your address and I'll send you theirs."

"What about . . . Carol?"

Ah, so it had been Carol that he'd wanted to know about. "Carol lost her heart to a policeman in Chicago. He's sold a horror book that Carol bravely read although it scared the liver out of her."

Tweed chuckled. "That's my Carol."

"Will you be there a while, down where you are now?"

The tone of his voice was firm with decision. "I think I've finally found my place."

"I'm so glad for you. It's taken you a while. Cray had a similar problem. It took him a while, too, but he realized Susanne is his 'place.'"

"Felicia, you and Salty have been very important to me. I could never begin to tell you how . . . secure you've made me feel all this while, knowing you two were there."

With great irony laced in her wonderful voice, she mentioned, "It would have been nice if we'd known where you were. It's been some strain trying to tell God where to look for you."

"I was never anywhere long enough. But this is the place."

"When did you know that?"

"It's a long story."

"Come home and tell it to us."

"Maybe you all could come down here."

"We could, almost anytime. Bob and Jo live in our attic and—"

"That attic was great! Tell Bob he's a smart man."

"Yes. Well, they're here, and we can take off, now and again, while they look after the kids."

"More kids?"

"A lovely bunch. You would be amazed by them. And you should know that Bob and Jo have a beautiful little redheaded boy."

"It doesn't surprise me that they have a kid already. What'd they name him?"

Felicia made the pronunciation just the right nudge. "Tweed Two."

There was a silence. Then a surprised but delighted Tweed said a satisfied, "Good."

When they'd finally said their goodbyes and hung up, Tweed looked at Sam and said, "I've told you about the Browns. One of them named a kid after me."

Sam said, "That was smart." His words held Tweed's same satisfied sound. Then Sam asked, "You going to the hospital again today?"

"Yeah." Tweed took a deep breath and looked out the window to the far horizon. "I don't think it does any good."

"Sanford thinks so."

Tweed looked back at Sam. "I feel so sorry for her. We call her Jane, like an anonymous Jane Doe, but we all wonder what her name can be. If we knew, we might get through to her. Calling her by another name isn't the trigger. I don't think her subconscious realizes we're trying to make contact."

"Try out names."

"The nurses have done that each separate time they go in her room. I wonder if she'll ever waken." Then he looked back at the horizon. "I wonder if she'll ever open her eyes and look at me."

Sam heard that. "Don't go falling for a Sleeping Beauty. She could have a husband and five kids. You'd just get underfoot."

"The man with her was a lot older." Tweed had stiffened a bit.

Sam frowned. "Watch out for yourself."

"Look. I'm only trying to help Sanford. I was the last one to talk to her."

And Sam said, "I wonder if anyone ever will again? Maybe if they found someone from before this happened, she could come out of it. Maybe your voice just reminds her of what happened."

"You got a point."

However, several days later, an alert citizen found an expensive purse just the other side of the border. It was a Coach purse and registered to Connie Moody. Such a theft from a Virginia woman was checked. No one knew exactly where she was, but she was traveling with her uncle Clyde in South Texas.

With the murders and a comatose female in a hospital who was unaccounted for, there was an investigation.

So, by that incident, they knew her name was Connie Moody before she ever wakened. The older man had been her uncle. They had been traveling together—and the sheriff knew, by then, that there had been more than two men involved in the capture of Clyde and Connie Moody in that isolated spot.

Connie was an orphan. But there were a whole slew of kin who came and sat and waited to see her and who worried about her and questioned Tweed.

"Where were you when all that happened to Connie, when they killed Uncle Clyde?"

Tweed replied, "Some long distance away."

"What were they doing in that awful old car?"

"I don't know."

But Connie's kin were from the crowded eastern coast, and they hadn't yet realized about unpeopled distances.

Tweed said, "Come to the window and look outside. Go to any window in this hospital and look to the horizon. See the landing strip? This is very isolated country."

A rather snotty male cousin of Connie's inquired, "How'd you happen to find her?"

Tweed was courteous. "She'd lit a tire to burn."

Gregory was surprised. "She had? Why did she do that?"

"So the black smudge smoke would call attention to the fact that somebody needed help."

Gregory considered such an act. "Now that's innovative. Did she take the tire off the car? Connie could do that."

"It was a spare."

"Why are you here?" They had all asked Tweed that and watched him. He did look like a highwayman of some woman's dream. But his blue eyes were steady and dismissive.

Tweed repeated his now-standard reply to Gregory, "I was the last person she talked to. We needed her name to find you all."

With a small, snide smile, Gregory commented, "I thought 'you all' was for a group, not one person."

"I implied that we needed to find all of you, her family. I wasn't talking about just you."

Gregory considered that and said in an enlightened way, "Oh, I see." And his attitude eased. He looked at Tweed differently.

And Tweed asked, "Has anyone had any response from her?"

"No." Gregory's voice was kinder. "She frowns just a tad, as if annoyed by us."

"Do her lips move at all?"

"Not that anyone's said." Gregory shifted and said with courtesy, "I don't know if anyone has remembered to thank you. I am impressed that you landed on that road, if anyone could label it a road."

"You went out there?"

"Yes. Just some of us. No women. We needed to see if there was anything that would tell us who had done that to Clyde and to Connie. We needed to know if Connie had gotten them all."

"Yeah. We looked, too." Then he said to the cousin, "So you think she killed the men?"

"Uncle Clyde was already dead." He shrugged. Then he added, "I must say that I'm impressed with the caliber of men out here. You really fit the mold, you Texans."

With some fine irony, Tweed said, "I was originally from Pennsylvania."

"Oh." Then Gregory smiled.

Gregory didn't know, then, that Tweed had lied. Tweed had no idea where his home place was. He'd been abandoned in a bus-stop rest room, in St. Louis, newly born.

Sanford came into the waiting room and saw Tweed standing by the window, talking with one of the Moodys. Sanford came over and said, "Can I see you for a minute?"

Gregory said, "Of course."

"Tweed." Sanford dismissed Gregory.

"Yeah."

The two walked out into the hall. Tweed said, "You don't need me here. I gotta get back. Sam needs me out at the place."

Sanford walked a pace or two; then he stopped and looked at Tweed. "You're the only one who gets any reaction from her. You haven't seen her yet today. Go in and say her real name to her. Do that. If she doesn't respond to you, we'll let you go for a couple of days."

"I think it's a waste of time. She probably relates my voice to what happened and—"

"She could relate your voice to her rescue. Think what she'd been through. She was alone, no means of escape, there was no one anywhere around. You handled those bodies. It had been at least twenty-four hours since they'd died. Think of her spending that night in that place, the only one left alive, not knowing what or who else might show up. And, now, we know that there'd been others who'd left there. She could well suppose that they might come back."

"Yeah."

"Just go in and hold her hand, say her name and tell her she's all right."

"I've held her hand and told her that every time. She doesn't come out of it."

"Don't give up."

So they went again to Connie's room. Tweed had never had a name to say to her before then. He took her hand and leaned over her. He said, "I'm Tweed Brown. Connie, do you hear me? You're safe."

Her lips parted, and he noted that they were healing. The stitch had been removed. He saw the bruise on her eye was the green of a healing bruise. She frowned and moved her head a little as if to raise it from water, or out of the submerged sleep that had engulfed her. Her fingers clenched his hand and she took an unsteady breath.

But she relaxed and her face smoothed. Her fingers were only curled around his hand.

Tweed frowned and was disappointed. He looked up at Sanford who was grinning ear to ear.

"See?" Sanford whispered the word as he motioned Tweed to come into the hall.

Tweed laid her hand carefully beside her and followed Sanford into the hall. He said quietly, "She didn't come out of it."

Sanford shook his head and said with exuberance, "That's the best yet!" Then he explained to Tweed, "She just isn't quite ready to face all the stress she'll have to deal with."

"I pity her." Tweed put his Stetson on. "No family. Well, there's that mob out in the waiting room. They're either wealthy or ne'er-do-wells."

"She's got guts." Sanford soothed. "But there she was, isolated, too far from anything. If she hadn't re-lit that tire, she'd of died there."

"She's something, all right. Any talk of a husband or boyfriend? Where'd she live? What'd she do?"

"She's just out of grad school. She's an accountant."

"Accountant?" Tweed was some dismayed. He'd had very little formal education.

"No husband," Sanford continued as if Tweed hadn't spoken. "The man she'd been seeing the most hasn't shown up, but he was informed."

"Sounds like she had a winner." Tweed was being sarcastic.

"I believe he's been in touch." Sanford studied Tweed through narrowed, thoughtful eyes. "Come back in two days. Please."

"Please? I didn't know you knew that word. I'll try, but you might put a little pressure on the boyfriend. She could use some male support through all this."

"Come back."

"Well, I could. I do have to keep tabs on Betty Lou."

"Stay away from Betty Lou."

"Are you waving that pretty blond comatose victim under my nose, hoping to distract me from Betty Lou? You must have a screw loose."

"I want Connie lucid. She reacts to your voice. I want you here until I can contact her by myself."

"Lucid." Tweed tasted the word.

"Awake, conscious."

"I see." Tweed stuck out his lower lip and nodded once.

"I want Connie to hear me."

"Getting possessive?"

"I hate a patient not to hear my directions and orders."

"Oh." Tweed nodded bobs. "It's control that you want."

"Yes."

Tweed grinned, slapped Sanford on the shoulder in a friendly way and said, "I'll mention you unkindly to Betty Lou."

Sanford took a breath.

"I'm ignoring your orders not to see Betty Lou. I'll be back the day after tomorrow, if I can get jarred loose from my duties at the ranch."

"The Moodys have offered to reimburse your wages for you to be here."

"You mean I can get *paid* to hold that sleeping woman's hand? Hot dang! There's other th— No. I didn't mean that."

Sanford put his hand on Tweed's shoulder. "You're a good man. I'm sorry Betty Lou can't have you. You'd make her a better husband. But I want her."

"What's she want?"

"She doesn't know yet, but she will choose wisely."

Tweed resettled his Stetson and said, "I'll tell Betty Lou that you gave me a recommendation."

Sanford said through threatening teeth, "You do, and I'll take out your appendix—from—the—left—side."

"I'm going to tell Betty Lou that you've been threatening to open up my stomach over her."

"She doesn't know I've chosen her, as yet. Don't smile. I could set your leg at an angle." Then Sanford smiled kindly.

Tweed laughed. "I'll have to go look at Betty Lou, and if she passes the tests, I'll have to find out if she could like a gimpy man."

"What tests?"

"Oh, I'll have to see if she likes her hair mussed a little and her clothes displaced."

In a deadly way, Sanford enunciated, "Don't do that."

Tweed looked innocent and guessed, "What? Stand here? Be earnest? Mess around with Betty Lou?"

"That's it."

"What a selfish man you are. Does Betty Lou know that?"

"She'll learn."

"I've been reading up on the male-female relationship, and cavemen are obsolete."

"She won't mind."

And Tweed laughed as he turned, lifted his hand to Sanford and walked away.

So Tweed went in search of Betty Lou. And he found her walking down the hall in another section on that floor. He stopped her and said, "Hi, beautiful."

"I know. It's such a burden." But she laughed, and that maddening dimple flickered in her cheek.

"Do you know Sanford is staking you out?"

"Really?"

"Now, honey, you can't be that dense. Do you know he's forbidden me to speak to you?"

"What do you have to say?"

"Well . . . for starters, he's a barbarian. You want a civilized man."

She moved her head and turned to look around the empty hall. "Are there any?" Betty Lou looked up at him in questioning interest. It was a little overdone.

He lectured her kindly, "You need a firm man's gentle hand on you to give you guidance. I'll volunteer."

"How gracious!"

"How about lunch? I find I'm free at this time. I can give you a different viewpoint on men in general and me in particular."

"I can't tell you how sorely tempted I am, but I had to go to lunch first call, and anyway, Sanford would probably be very tart with me if I did anything so rash as that...with you. He's so jealous of you that he gnashes his teeth if I even say your name."

"Good. We'll make him sweat."

"Now, Tweed, you know I can't distress him."

He was astonished. "Why not?" He spread out his arms. "You get married and you're off limits."

"Honey, Sanford hasn't mentioned marriage?" She did the questioning statement typical of Texans. "I'm still working on that."

Tweed was logical. "Let's scare him."

"You're wicked. Do you realize that?"

He shook his head in agitation. "God, I sure try."

"Run along now, and quit tempting me."

"It's nice to know you're not revolted."

"Honey, if I wasn't already snared, I'd be after you like a bee after a honey pot."

He put his hand on his chest and took a steadying breath. "Now who's wicked?"

That dimple flickered, and she turned around and left him standing there, but he got to watch her doing it.

Tweed had a thoughtful ride back to the ranch. When he got there and stopped the car, Sam came out on the porch. He stood and watched Tweed's tired exit from the car. Then he watched as Tweed stretched his good muscles as he looked off toward the horizon.

Sam said, "You going back tomorrow?"

"No, the day after. Sanford begged."

"Take the plane when you go. You're wasting time driving it."

"I'd appreciate it." Tweed climbed the steps to the porch, his boots clumping. He stood and looked around. Then he asked, "What do you know about women?"

"Some woman tempting you?"

"Avoiding me."

"Who?"

"That little Betty Lou. Sanford has her staked out, and she doesn't mind."

"Your problem is that you didn't get sick when you should have. He has propinquity on his side."

"What the hell's that?"

"He's there."

"Yeah."

"They have a lot in common. She'll understand his profession. If she married you and was out here, she'd die of loneliness. She needs people."

"Now, how did you know that? You been studying on finding yourself another wife. You done wore out one."

"No. I've been looking for you a wife."

"Me!"

Sam gestured to show openness. "I want you to stay around. You could become a drifter. I think you have it in you to stay put and build yourself a nice life."

Tweed grinned fondly at his mentor. Sam had taken Tweed seriously ever since he'd answered Sam's advertisement for a manager. Without very much formal education, Tweed knew men and animals, and he could fix anything.

Tweed walked slowly over to the porch rail and leaned one hip against it. He looked at Sam with some caution. Sam was hunting a wife for him? "Who have you checked out?"

"I just started. I have a way to go yet."

With some hesitation, Tweed mentioned, "You and me might not see women... the same. You might get me someone who'll turn out wrong, and I'd be miserable... or she would be."

"I've been paying attention. I know just what you need."

Very carefully, Tweed asked, "What?"

"A woman."

"Well, that's a given. Women are all we have available to be wives."

Sam was determined. "The right one would be good for you."

"I don't mind going into town."

"No. You need permanence. A good woman. One who'll make a family."

"Where would we live?"

"Here." Sam gestured openly. "There's room enough."

"My bed squeaks."

"If you're going to be rowdy, you can get out of bed and down on the floor."

"It can get pretty cold here, winters."

"Well—" Sam sighed gustily "—I suppose I can cough up enough for a new solid bed."

And Tweed laughed. But he looked fondly at Sam.
"You're a good man."

Sam's eyes twinkled. "Because I'm trying to find
you a willing woman?"

"Because you're a good man."

"So are you, Tweed. And don't you forget that.
Don't ever sell yourself short. Or cheap."

Tweed stood up and stretched again, moving his
body. "What do you suppose would be a reasonable
offer to consider from some eager woman who can't
wait to clean this house, move Jake out so she can
cook and do the dishes and sleep with me?"

"Oh, you ought not consider anything less than a
hundred thousand."

Tweed laughed.

Sam grinned and said, "They've run that bunch of
strays into the corral. Tell me what you think of
them."

"You know, we ought to give Hugo part of the
range and leave him alone. During the season, we
ought to give him all the cows he can handle and build
up a herd of his."

Sam had heard the "we ought to—" and it pleased
him. He questioned, "Leave him be?"

"Yeah."

"Tempts a man to live that way, doesn't it?"

"Breeding?"

"Ahh." Sam sighed and smiled. "To be that young
and single-minded. No. Having control. That's what
Hugo wants."

"He *is* thinking of breeding or he wouldn't be
stealing your cows."

"That's to establish his base," Sam explained.
"Now, don't grin. A despot needs subjects. Hugo

needs a herd. He is willing to help out in that phase of the operation, but he mainly needs a herd that will follow him.''

"He protects his cows. He hides them and threatens the wolves and coyotes and us over them. The cows belong to him. He probably has names for each of them in that evil little brain. But he herds those cows to water and to good grass.''

Sam agreed. ''That's part of it all. For their obedience, he protects.''

''Now do you mean to tell me that old Hugo hasn't the voracious sex drive I thought? That he just does it as a means to control? I find I *am* disillusioned.''

Sam laughed.

It was then that Tweed looked at Sam for a while before he asked, ''Would you mind if Salty and Felicia came to visit? They'd like to see me, and I sure would like you to meet them. Could they stay here?''

Sam looked surprised. ''Sure. How come you needed to ask?''

Very touched, Tweed looked down and smiled a little as he nodded a couple of short nods. Then he reset his hat and said, ''I'll go look at those beeves.''

''Supper at five.''

''What?'' Tweed was going down the steps and didn't turn around.

''Stew.''

By then, Tweed was far enough away that the older man wouldn't be able to see the moisture in his eyes. Quite natural sounding, he managed, ''Stew? What a surprise!''

And Sam chuckled.

# Three

Two days after that, Tweed flew to the hospital and was greeted by the Moodys, who were still holding down the waiting room. An aunt exclaimed, "When they turned her over the last time, she said, 'Ummmm.'"

Tweed inquired, "'s that good?"

It was Gregory who explained, "It's the first sound she's made since we came here."

Tweed didn't tell them about Connie saying the drawn out "Oh, no," to him that first time. It sounded too much like she was rejecting him. If the Moodys thought that, they might object to him going into her room.

So he went on down the hall and met Sanford coming out of another room.

Sanford greeted Tweed by saying, "Glad to see you.

Keep away from Betty Lou. She told me you hunted her down the last time you were here."

"She's using me to make you jealous. Are you jealous of me?"

"Hell, yes."

Closemouthed, Tweed laughed in his throat. Then he inquired, "How's the sleeping beauty?"

"She liked being turned over this last time."

"Did she say anything?"

"No. Just a sound."

Tweed took a deep breath and said, "Well, let's see if she can do better than that."

Tweed washed his hands as usual, and went to the bedside. He leaned over and took Connie's hand. Looking into her sleeping face, he said, "Hello, Connie, it's Tweed. It's time to open those eyes so I can see what color they are. Wake up."

Her eyelids shimmered quivers, and she lifted her chin a little. Her hand held his.

He coaxed, "Now how's a man supposed to know a woman who doesn't open her eyes? Look at me, Sleeping Beauty. Wake up."

She struggled to obey. Her mouth worked gently, as if seeking the words she needed, and her eyelashes appeared to blink against strong light.

Tweed watched her. Then he said in a normal voice to Stanford, "Doctor, is the light too strong in here?"

"It might be. Let me close the blinds by her head."

He did that with dispatch, and the blinds clattered.

Connie's body jerked with the sound, and Tweed soothed, "The doctor is just closing the blinds a little so it isn't so bright."

Connie said, "Thank you."

Tweed told Sanford, "She said thank you."

She pressed his hand and pulled it toward her just slightly. Then again she struggled to say the words, "Thank...you."

Tweed replied gently, "You're welcome."

But she was again sunk into sublevel escape.

Tweed asked Sanford in a normal voice, "Did you hear her?"

"Yes. This is a great stride. She not only knows you, she realizes how she came to know you."

Tweed considered the careful choice of Sanford's words, used in case Connie could hear him. The words acknowledged all the horror that had taken place without underlining any of it.

Tweed tried again, saying to Connie, "You know you're safe here at the hospital? You're healing. The bruises are lightening."

Sanford frowned and brushed his hand aside in a gesture that asked Tweed to stop talking.

Tweed nodded to Sanford. "Connie, do you know I work on a ranch about fifty miles from here? I flew in today in order to see you again."

Her lips moved and she smiled. It was slight, but it was a smile.

Quite smug, Tweed looked up at Sanford.

Sanford smiled, and his eyes looked somewhat bleary.

Tweed said, "My boss loaned me his plane. It's the one I used to rescue you."

Sanford frowned furiously at Tweed.

Connie's hand tightened on Tweed's.

"You know you're safe here. Nothing can harm you ever again. I promise."

She smiled just a tiny bit.

And yet again, Tweed said, "Wake up, Connie. It's time for you to wake up."

For days, everyone in the hospital had been saying that to her, and they had probably caught her attention in that sublevel vacuum she was inhabiting, but it was Tweed's order that she heard. Slowly her eyes opened. And she looked at him.

"Hi." He was intent. "Your eyes are brown."

She said, "Yes."

"Want some water?"

"Yes."

Sanford quickly put a glass with a straw into Tweed's hand.

Tweed held the glass low by the side of her head as she sipped from the bendable straw, and he told her, "This is your doctor. His name is Sanford."

She looked at the indicated man.

Sanford said, "Hi, Connie. You're doing fine. You're okay."

She looked back at Tweed. She released the straw from her mouth and said seriously, "Your eyes are really blue."

He nodded.

"I...I...I...remember."

"You're okay now."

She shivered.

Tweed looked at Sanford. "A blanket?"

Like a directed orderly, Sanford got the blanket. He spread it over Connie and tucked the blanket around her. "Don't worry about anything. You're in good health. You're all right. A lot of your family is here."

She was clinging to Tweed's hand. But she did listen. She looked at Tweed and questioned, "Tweed?"

"Yep. I'm named after a coat."

She considered that seriously.

"I've had a lot of names. I was abandoned in a bus-stop rest room just after I was born."

Sanford said, "I hadn't known that."

"I hadn't mentioned it." Then he said to Connie, "I'll show you the coat if you'll get up and walk out of this room."

She tried.

Sanford said, "Maybe tomorrow or the next day."

And Tweed told Connie, "The coat'll wait. Somebody said you're married with five kids, is that right?"

Her eyes twinkled a little. "No." It was said softly.

"Well, if there isn't some man who's in charge of you, you could count on me for a time."

With some amused irony, she said a droll, "Thank you."

"You have to realize I can't sit in the waiting room with that passel of kinfolk you've got out there?" That was the questioning do-you-understand statement. "I'm a gofer at a ranch that's fifty miles down the road, I told you that, and getting here and back is a chore when I have chores to do out there."

Sanford gazed at Tweed fascinated. Tweed was minimizing himself. He was allowing the woman to believe he was nothing. Sanford had never realized how careful Tweed could be. Then Sanford listened as Tweed went on.

"My boss is a good man, and he's allowed me to check up on you. Like I said, he loaned me the plane today to come to the hospital. But I can't impose on him too much. So if I'm not here, dancing attendance, you'll know I'm out hunting a recalcitrant cow, or a muleheaded horse, or pitchforking—hay. Understand?"

That tiny smile came back, and she nodded minutely.

"So, until I can come back and take control, I expect you to behave, get on your feet, eat what you want and pay attention. Understand?"

The smile sparkled in her eyes. "Yes, sir."

Tweed squinted his eyes and commented, "Those were the right words to reply to me, but the sound is lacking the proper amount of respect. You ought to work on that."

To that, she replied, "Yes . . . SIR!"

"That's marginally better. Is there any other man you want informed of your whereabouts?"

She shook her head a tiny tremor as she continued to watch his face.

Tweed went on: "Sanford is a good doctor. Do most of what he tells you."

Sanford said a complaining, "Most?"

"He's got a bad case on a nurse, named Betty Lou, and he won't even let me speak to her. See if you can straighten him out."

Sanford groaned.

So, having given Connie something else to think about, and introducing her to a toehold in the gossip around the hospital, he said, "I'll see you in a couple of days." He lifted her hand and kissed *his* thumb, which was lying on the back of her hand. Then he grinned at her.

Sanford said to Connie, "I'll make sure he leaves."

Soberly, Tweed explained, "He's terrified Betty Lou will try to waylay me."

There was an amused sound in Connie's throat.

Supremely satisfied, Tweed put on his Stetson at the door as he walked out into the hall, followed by Sanford.

Tweed turned to Sanford and said, "That'll be just a tad over two thousand dollars."

"What is?"

"Professional expenses. The trip here by plane, my valuable time." He gestured, opening out his hand. "My Waking Sleeping Beauties demonstration."

With a long-suffering sigh, Sanford told the ceiling, "I'll probably never hear the last of this—" he looked at Tweed "—from you."

Tweed nodded thoughtfully. "That's a firm possibility."

"You did a good job. What a charmer."

"Let's go find Betty Lou, and I'll demonstrate how to get around her upbringing. I'm on a roll, if you'll pardon the expression."

"Tweed," Sanford warned.

Tweed shrugged. "Okay. Do it your way. Wait."

"You kissed your own thumb."

"That's the teaser. That makes 'em anxious." He resettled his Stetson and looked down the hall from under the brim.

"Tweed, thanks for coming. You were the only one who could reach her."

Tweed shook his head in denial. "I was a link. Either she'd get the horrors, hearing from me, or she'd need me as a connection to begin from so that she could go on."

"I understand, but I'm impressed you understand that."

"I've been around a long, hard time."

"But you've survived."

Tweed agreed. "At a crucial time in my life, I was given to the Browns in Temple, Ohio. I didn't stay long, but they have influenced all of my conduct since I've known them."

"I'd like to hear about it."

Tweed dismissed such a confidence. "Sometime."

Sanford explained carefully, "I deal with kids who are troubled by circumstances. If you have any advice or direction that could help such kids, I'd be very grateful. These kids are like you must have been. They have no impairment, just bad circumstances."

"Yeah."

"If ever you want to talk, I'm here."

"Thanks."

Sanford clarified his invitation. "I mean to talk about being a kid with problems. To give me help. You are the most confident man I've ever known. You're far beyond me in practical wisdom. I wish I had your knack with communication."

Tweed groaned. "Oh, Sanford, how can't you recognize envy?"

Quite earnestly, Sanford asked, "For what?"

Tweed slapped his friend's shoulder with affection and said, "You can't be that dense." Tweed resettled his Stetson yet again and said, "I've got to be getting back. If you should need another patient consultation, don't hesitate to call."

And the doctor watched as Tweed walked off down the empty hall, whispering loudly for him to hear, "Betty Lou? Betty Lou?"

Sam's plane flew like a dream. It was wonderful to be in the air and seeing far. It made Tweed feel like a god. Well. One of the minor ones.

He landed at the ranch and put the plane away in the hangar. He removed a small but vital part, and hung it and the key on the hidden board. He took the ignition key from the board and walked over to the Jeep to drive it back to the house. Sam would be curious.

They sat at the kitchen table as Jake made them peel potatoes, and Tweed told them Connie had wakened. "I gave Sanford a bill for just over two thousand for my Waking the Sleeping Beauty demonstration."

Jake, especially, loved that. "How'd you do it? You kiss her? Isn't that how the Prince woke Sleeping Beauty?"

"Well, now, Jake, I haven't been reading any fairy tales—"

Jake protested, "I remember them from—"

"Yesterday?"

Jake chuffed, "Keep it up, keep it up and you get no supper!"

"So, frog, you need to know I didn't kiss her. I just said it was time for her to wake up."

"You told her." Jake turned from the sink to clarify that.

Tweed grinned. "Well, you gotta know everyone's been telling her that all along, and I just happened to say it at the right time."

Sam guessed, "She knew your voice from just before she went out of it."

"That could be."

"What'd she say?"

"Not much. But she opened her eyes, she smiled a little and she tried to get out of bed."

"Why?"

"I told her I was named for a coat and if she'd hop out of bed, I'd let her see it."

Sam's eyes crinkled. "That old coat?"

"It's a symbol to me. When you meet Salty, you'll understand."

"I look forward to knowing him."

Then Tweed said to Jake, "And he's a decent cook. Learned in the navy."

"So'd I!" Jake turned belligerent.

Tweed said to Sam, "I can't wait for them to meet. It'll be like two comets. We'll have to arrange so it's outside. Hey, Jake, did you know Salty was a prize-fighter in the navy?"

"That Salty Brown?"

"The one and only," Tweed agreed.

"Jeeezzz, man, I heard of him."

All the time, Sam was watching Tweed. "Something happened there, today, what was it?"

Tweed considered. "Nothing particular."

"If you figure it out, tell me."

Tweed shrugged.

One of the things about Connie being awake during the day was that Tweed got to go into her room alone. He took off his Stetson, put it on a chair and went to her bed. She was propped up with pillows. She had on a yellow bed jacket that was made from some kind of material, like . . . silk?

Tweed tried to remember if he'd ever actually seen silk.

He told her, "You're looking better."

"Than . . . what?"

"Well, you're cleaner, your bruises are fading, your eyes are open. You look wide-awake with those brown dots for your eyes. You're looking good."

Her blond hair tended to wave and ducktail. It was a little tumbled. She looked like a woman in bed, waiting for some man to roll her around. He'd better not mention that.

He asked, "How're you feeling?"

"All right."

"All that mob of people still hanging around?"

"Only an aunt and one cousin."

"That—Gregory?"

"You know Greg?"

Tweed considered. "He isn't a Greg. You have to call him by the full name."

"You think he's a snob."

Tweed examined the thought. "Yeah. That about covers it."

"He's very kind."

"He's probably fixing to marry you."

"He has mentioned that."

"You willing?"

She looked out the window, her brown eyes sad. "He was very brave to offer."

"Brave?"

Pensively, she added, "After what happened."

"You spooky about men now? It was only those men. There are other men that would be a lot of fun."

The word fell flat. "Fun."

"Now, don't tell me you were a virgin," he chided.

She nodded a couple of slow times very sadly.

"Well." He paced over to the window and looked out; then he turned back to her and said, "I don't think they probably showed much consideration or finesse—" he was back to looking out the window to allow her the privacy from his observation "—but there are men who can do it in a much nicer way."

Bitterly, she replied, "So they say."

He turned and looked at her seriously. She was watching him. He smiled a little. "I believe your uncle Tweed could give you a demonstration that would carry you through this crisis."

She gasped.

He lifted up his hands and turned his head to one side. "No. No. Don't thank me. It's my duty as a man to show you what you'd be missing if you give up on the more intimate—and certainly more *interesting*—side of social intercourse."

She stuttered a word and looked appalled by him.

And he had the audacity to then say, "First a greeting kiss. That's the lesson for today."

He leaned over. Her brown eyes were enormous, her lips parted, and she was pressed back into the pillows. She frowned and jerked her head ... and he gently kissed her forehead.

He drew back and said, "That wasn't so bad, was it?"

Great, big tears gathered in pools at the bottom of her eyes, and one spilled over.

He watched it, leaning closer; then he said, "How'd you do that? Here it comes. It needs to be kissed." And he kissed that tear. Then he leaned away from her so that he could watch avidly. "Squeeze out another, so's I can kiss your other cheek."

She put her hand to her head and gulped with her emotion, but even as she shook her head, she smiled a little. She said, "I'm not quite stable yet. They gave me something. It makes me feel odd."

He protested, "Well, kissing you makes me feel real strange. It's like sniffing glue."

She was censorious. "When did you sniff glue?"

"I don't ever recall doing something like that, but kissing must be close. Is your lip healed, or do I need to kiss it well?"

That was a test. If she said it was healed, which it was, then he would know that she didn't want to be kissed.

She felt her lip and said, "It's better."

He moved his head closer to hers. "Want it well?"

"You're pushy, do you know that?"

He squinted his eyes and considered. "Nobody's ever complained about it."

She laughed and put a hand up to almost touch his hair. Then she stopped, put her hand back down and just watched him.

So he straightened and grinned at her. She wasn't sure she wanted to be kissed, but she had flirted enough that he wasn't discouraged from trying another time.

And she encouraged him to talk. "What did you do these last few days?"

"Just like I told you. It all happened. I had to find a muleheaded horse, deal with a recalcitrant cow and fork...hay."

"Where do you fork the...hay?" She used his own pause exactly.

"I clean out the stable."

She didn't believe him for a minute.

He grinned. "Actually, I did have to deal with that...horse. But the recalcitrant cow is a computer. Sam's going modern on us and really shaking up the entire system. I prefer the simple life."

"I know computers."

"Wanna come out and get us familiar? Oh, no, no, no. Not what you're thinking, you hussy. Familiar with the computer!" His eyes teased her.

"They're easy."

"Hah!"

So he'd given the orphan with the hovering relatives something else to think about and anticipate...if she wanted to do it. She could always decline to go with him and teach Sam and maybe even him how to work the silent, useless computer.

And it would be so interesting to see how Gregory handled it if she should actually choose to go out to the Fuller ranch.

Tweed went back home and said to Sam, "I invited the woman, Connie Moody, to come out here and teach us the computer."

"Did you now?"

"Yep. You can afford it, and it will make this whole operation easier to cope with. You're a martinet. You push. She'll be a kinder, gentler despot." He paused to survey Sam. "And she'd be easier to look at."

He replied, "Hah!"

Tweed reiterated, "She is, you old warthog."

And Jake said, "Bring her out for a look over."

Tweed replied, "If I do, you have to behave."

Jake was indignant.

And Tweed said, "No touching."

Jake retorted, "That goes for *you*, too!"

Sam laughed, "Har, har, har!"

And later Jake told Tweed, "You're good for the old man. He was so—quiet—for all those years. I hadn't heard him laugh, not in all those years, like he does now, with you, like he did tonight."

"Sam's one of the best."

"That he is."

"Jake?"

"Yeah?"

"He's been lucky all these years that he had you around. You're a good man."

"Ah, Tweed."

Then in a rush, Tweed teased, "I'll be glad when Salty comes down and teaches you how to cook." And he ducked out of the door fast enough.

So the next time Tweed went to the hospital, Connie was up, sitting in a chair. Her family had supplied her with some of her own things from Virginia. She had on a pale tangerine satin-and-lace, man-killing negligee.

Any woman wearing something like that expected some comment. "That one of Victoria's Secrets? Or is it from Victoria's closet?"

"Now how does a man know about Victoria's Secrets?"

"That catalogue is right up there with *Playboy* and Sears's underwear section."

And she laughed. She really did.

His eyes hot and amused, Tweed watched her. He lounged on the bottom of her bed, and she sat in the chair. He talked to her about the quirks of computers, horses and cattle, but he never touched her and he didn't kiss even her hand.

He got off the bed, picked up his hat and said, "You ought to be out of here soon. Want to fly out to our place and give it a once-over? You wouldn't have to make up your mind right away. Sanford says you could fly out in another day or two and then come back here. Sort of a patient leave. Or a trial run. How about it?"

And she said, "All right."

"You're in for a treat. It's a wonderful place. Not very close to anything. But we have a computer that's a fine challenge."

"Day after tomorrow."

"I'll come for you early. I'll be here just after dawn. The cook, Jake, has fixed up a bed for you to sleep. You can look around all you want. With the operation that Sam runs, there're mostly males out there, but they're all good men. We'll see how it goes and, Connie, we'll take good care of you."

"Betty Lou said you would, but her dimple kept flickering in and out. How much can I trust her?"

He looked off and considered before he said gravely, "Well, with Betty Lou, it helps that you're female. If you were male, I don't believe I could give you a serious reply."

So the two days later, Tweed did arrive just after dawn. And Connie was ready.

"Got everything?" Tweed smiled at her. She had on a blue dress that fit her nice body just right. She had a slithery, wild scarf for her hair. She wore high heels and hose, and she carried a jacket against the morning chill.

He asked carefully, "Been shopping?"

"My eldest aunt did the shopping for me. She thought I was going back to Virginia. She hadn't known that I was planning a trip out into the countryside with you."

"And you were reluctant to ask her to shop again?"

"She's very dear."

He understood that Connie was.

She picked up a Stetson of her own from a chair and said, "I'm ready."

"Only one day?"

"No. Two." She indicated a sling bag that held enough for that time.

He grinned widely and nodded in satisfaction. "Come on, woman, the day's getting away from us."

She looked at her watch in disbelief.

They went down, out of the hospital, with the staff calling all sorts of things to their departing guest. "Be careful of him." That one was shushed right away. "Have fun!" That one was frowned on by others. But Connie only waved back and smiled.

"You're doing great." Tweed gave her a pleased look.

"I am really grateful for the respite from the hospital."

"We can handle that."

But as they got to the plane, there stood Gregory! He had an overnight case with him, and he smiled.

# Four

Tweed looked at Gregory as if he were some sort of cattle tick. The look was a distasteful concentration on how to get rid of him.

Connie inquired, "Where are you going?" She considered Gregory with polite interest.

Gregory smiled smoothly as if he held the high hand. "Along."

"Where?" Tweed, too, was polite.

"With you two." Gregory appeared to believe his company would make the trip into a cheerful, companionable jaunt. "I'd like to see a working cattle ranch while I'm down here. I might even invest a little."

"Invest?"

"Cash. I understand most of Texas is under a financial hammer."

Tweed snorted. First Tweed said, "You always write or say TEXAS in caps." And then he said, "Sonny, there is no way that you can go along."

"Oh, but I shall."

"How?" Tweed watched the man.

"With you."

"I have about the smallest plane made that will carry two people. Are you planning to ride on one wing?"

"Hire another plane."

"This plane's ours." Tweed let that soak in. "I have to take it back." Then he said, "I do have a suggestion. If you're dead set on going, rent a car and I'll draw you a map."

Gregory's face was still. "You own the plane?"

"I don't. It's a working plane and belongs to the ranch. I get to use it if I'm behaving reasonably."

Connie inquired, "Do you behave...unreasonably?"

"At times." He didn't move his head from his contemplation of the intruder, but he moved his eyes to give her a weighing glance. He wanted her to think this was one of those times when he wouldn't be reasonable.

He would fool her. He was going to be so polite that she'd probably gnash her teeth in irritation. She had said nothing about Gregory going along, and she had made no comment on the limited space in the plane.

Oh, of course. She had known the size of the plane. He only then recalled that she'd ridden to the hospital in it. And he was impressed because she surely would have recalled the plane's limited space.

Did it bother her, knowing that she would be that enclosed, with him? She hadn't refused to go. She had known about the size of the plane, and she hadn't commented on it at all. Maybe she didn't want Gregory along any more than he did.

Then Tweed thought that perhaps she didn't mind being close to him—and under his guidance and direction—providing he was subtle about it. If she appeared to have control and could back away, she would be all right. Maybe the shivering attacks hadn't given her the willies about all men, only the men responsible for the assaults.

Could she be that strong? He looked from Connie to Gregory, who was a pushy man. He was trying his best to include himself and be with Connie. He lacked finesse. He wasn't the man for Connie. He wouldn't be good for her. He had no soul. He was self-directed and thought he knew everything and just bullied his way into places he wasn't wanted. He was not for Connie.

So Tweed didn't ask her opinion. He took her to the mosquito they'd used before and he put her inside. He asked Gregory, "Do you have some paper?"

"Yes." Gregory reached into his inside jacket pocket and drew out a slender black book and a pen.

Tweed thought: Wouldn't you know Gregory would have a pen and blank paper? Naturally. Gregory would be one who was always prepared for whatever happened. He wouldn't have to contrive an alternative, he would have the solution. And Tweed decided that it would be very boring for Connie to endure someone that prosaic. But Tweed then had to resist testing to see for what all Gregory was actually prepared. Survival kit? Gas shortage? Rain?

He looked at the sky. He already knew what the weather would be. He'd known that two days ago. It would be the usual wonderful TEXAS weather.

Tweed opened the slender book and took the pen. He said, "You are here." He made a big *X*. "See this road? You take it for fifty miles, thataway." He pointed minimally with the top of Gregory's handy pen before he continued earnestly, "It's called the Comstock Road." And that *was* how it was called by all the old-timers. Somehow, Tweed forgot to mention it was listed as County Road One. "You can't miss the ranch. It's the only entrance there. Be sure to close the gate. It's a snap." Tweed meant the gate snapped.

Tweed smiled and said kindly to Gregory, "Step away, over yonder, so you don't get the prop wash. Drive carefully." He took off his Stetson and stored it as he got into the plane and put on the headphones, clicking switches and talking into the mouthpiece, ignoring Gregory.

Tweed said, "Jimmy, we got a circling buzzard wanting to roost?" Tweed continued, "Would you be so kind as to spread the word, courteously. Maybe Sig could waylay it." He set the mosquito in motion and eased it around to the runway, talking to the hospital's tower.

Connie didn't say one word. They went to the end of the runway and got permission to take off, and she just rode along, looking around.

They had gotten into the air and were putting along when she said, "So Gregory is a circling buzzard."

"Uh-huh."

It surprised her that he didn't hedge. "Did you think you would fool me?"

"No, ma'am. I thought, if I was subtle, you could pretend to be surprised when he doesn't show up."

"You're turning west."

"Have to, if we're going to get to the ranch."

"You sent him east."

"Hell, honey, if he's such a greenhorn that he can't tell which way the sun rises and sets, he has a serious problem."

"You never mentioned your ranch was west of the hospital. You do know he was out to the site of where... the... assault took place."

"Yeah." She'd actually made reference to the assault! He was so touched by that. He said, "Pointing east was a risk. But he may not realize the ranch borders the area where I found you. He rode west with somebody else and probably didn't pay attention to landmarks and other vital things a man notices in order to get from one place to another."

"You're sly," she accused.

He sighed. "I do try."

And she laughed!

So Tweed relaxed.

She commented, looking at him, "I believe that the most surprising thing about you is that you're completely honest."

Looking around the sky, keeping track of things and landmarks, he assured Connie, "All TEXANS are honest. I'm not a real, actual one, but I've been here for some years and the water changes a nonnative. Sam and I discussed that fact, and he claims that's so. It's the water."

"If I should stay awhile, then I would also become a native?"

"Honey, you could leave the day after tomorrow—after your visit with us is over—and the *state* would never let you forget that you're claimed. You'd probably find yourself subscribing to *Texas Monthly* just to keep in touch. You'd be startled by all the displaced TEXANS who wait by their mailboxes so's they can get that magazine and catch up on things."

"You make it sound like an incurable disease."

Looking around, he gave a nod and agreed, "It *is* similar." And as he tilted his head to look up and back, he said, "If I should really kiss you, you probably wouldn't even have to subscribe to *TM.*"

"Lord'a mercy!" she exclaimed; then she gasped and questioned in horror, "Did you hear that? My speech pattern is changing! Glory be!"

"Honey, you're from Virginia? That's not enough of a verbal difference from TEXAS, although we do have some quirky speech."

"Do you mean, I can . . . be absorbed?"

"Yep. It's part of the whole scheme. You'll probably get a craving for chew-y ta-bac-ca next."

"Ugh."

"Well, it isn't *required* at all. It'll just be the need to spit, as chewers do, to sort of accent things said. Without tobacco, you run out of spit."

She groaned and put a hand to her head. "I'm not sure I'm strong enough, yet, to become a TEXAN."

"We'll go slow." And he grinned at her so wickedly that she felt a lick of desire through her lower body. That sobered her in some shock. How could that be? How could she be sexually attracted after—And her mind refused to follow along her thinking. She stared from the window down onto the unpopulated, mesquite-covered ground.

She saw roads. There was a paved highway. There were dirt tracks. There were people around if there were roads. It wasn't entirely as isolated as— And again, her mind shunned thinking.

It was a pretty flight. It was the end of September, by then, and while the nights had cooled down, the days were summer days. They got to the ranch in a relatively short time.

There was a wind sock hanging from a pole to indicate the direction of the wind. They circled the necessary portion of the field to accommodate the breeze, but they didn't have to buzz the landing area in order to clear any grazers out of the way. And they landed on the natural ground. No runway.

But there was a hangar for the plane. It was big, metal and neat. They taxied to it, and Connie saw there were a couple of other planes stored inside, on a concrete floor. One plane was being worked on.

Sam was there.

He came to the plane as the dust blew away, and he opened the door for Connie. His eyes sparkled as he said, "Welcome to our place. I know you don't remember me, Connie, but I came to see you at the hospital. Since Tweed took you there, I had to be sure they were taking good care of you."

It was interesting, to Connie, that Tweed and now Sam had no compunction about discussing the assault. Everyone else was careful. She looked at Sam's bland face and saw that he was judging her sand. She couldn't appear a wimp to such a man, so she just said, "Thank you."

"Why?" Sam asked, tilting his head and waiting.

"For lending Tweed the plane to come to the hospital to visit me." She paused and looked at the empty landscape. Then she added, "He made me come back, you know. He wouldn't let me stay where I'd gone."

"That's a good way of explaining unconsciousness from trauma." So Sam wouldn't let her just tiptoe around what had happened to her. Then he took her arm and indicated the expanse of land and sky and mesquite trees. "This is as good as it gets."

While she did consider the area, she said, "You should see the hills of Virginia." She looked at him, then, with eyes that held amusement.

"I have." And Sam just left it at that as he tugged her arm to lead her toward the reasonably clean red Jaguar.

"No Jeep?"

He scoffed, "They're for peasants."

In a commanding voice, Tweed urged, "Let me drive!"

"If you want to drive, go get the Jeep."

"Ah-h-h." She gave Tweed a saucy glance.

He sighed as he agreed, "Sam thinks I'm a peasant. But if you value your life, don't get into any car he's driving."

So Sam asked Connie, "Would you like to drive the Jag?"

"I'd *love* to drive a Jaguar!"

"You got it. Here's the keys. After you let me off at the house, you can drive it as long as you're here. We got our own gas pump. Tweed'll show you how to fill the car's tank. Be sure to check the water in the radiator."

She mused over the words. "As long as I'm here? What if I should just move in?"

"Yep. Damn. I've committed the Jag to you for life, if you should decide to stay."

Her laugh was delicious to all the male ears within hearing distance. Actually, there were a surprising number of hands who'd appeared, around and about, having found the darnedest chores nearby. One hand was checking out the secure metal sheeting on the hangar. Another was clipping the scant weeds along the base.

As Connie drove toward the house, another hand was even working on the fence posts along the road to the house. It was Dusty who was spraying oil to discourage termites on the posts.

How many times had Sam told Dusty that it was time to do that?

Apparently that day was "the time." Dusty grinned wide and watched Connie drive past him. Sam put his arm on the back of the front seat and turned around to look back, and Dusty was still watching.

Sam's glance then fell on Tweed, who was sitting sideways in the cramped back seat, and Sam smiled a smug smile.

In sober deliberation, Tweed commented, "You're an old horny toad."

Sam then complained to Connie, "I get no respect here."

Tweed replied, "That's 'cause everybody knows how you think."

And Sam's amused eyes turned to consider Tweed. "Do you now?"

"Yep."

Sam then said to Connie, "The ranch is in the doldrums now, and Tweed is free to show you around this remarkable place. You need to see it all to understand this really is Paradise. I want you to see that not all of TEXAS is a horror spot."

"Thank you."

"Do you ride a horse?" Sam inquired courteously.

"You ask a Virginia woman that?"

"Well, there might be a Virginia lady who doesn't ride. You look like such a flower, I can't believe those little wrists could control a horse."

Cautiously, she inquired, "Is the horse ridable?"

"Sweet as sugar." Sam smiled benignly.

"Sugar?" Tweed questioned. "You're going to let her ride Sugar?"

"Yeah."

"Well, I'll be damned."

And Sam said, "More than likely."

With just the slightest hesitation, Connie asked, "Is this Sugar a rodeo horse?"

Tweed assured her, "She's just like her name. But you do need to take along a goodly supply of sugar cubes because otherwise she won't leave you alone."

Sam chuckled in his throat. "Just like a woman."

The multipeaked house was an added-to sprawl. It was of wood, plain and sturdy and painted white. It hadn't been painted in a while, but it wasn't tacky. Sam got out of the car and observed the house. He said, "We ought to paint it."

Tweed had exited the car, telling Connie to hold still. He'd gone around and opened the door for her. He helped her out as he, too, looked at the house. "Not in these next two days."

"You got plans?"

"I won't tolerate you getting Connie up on a ladder, painting, when she's a guest for these next two days. After that—if you can convince her to stay over—you can try to get her to paint the house."

"That sounds fair enough." Sam considered it. Then he complained, "But she's probably the kind that paints and then has to stand back and study the strokes. We'd have to put up such a deep scaffold for her to do that and we'd never get through!"

A chuckle went around inside Connie's chest. She asked Tweed, "Does Sam tease like this all the time?"

"He's being polite now. When he knows you, it gets really bad. He's just keeping it reined in so's you won't run back to the hospital for sanctuary."

Again.

As they walked up onto the porch, that's what all three thought. She had had desperate need of a sanctuary, and it had been a hospital. Tweed bit his lower lip and exchanged an anguished look with Sam.

She said, "This is the sanctuary. What a wonderful house. This porch is perfect. I love Tex—Sorry, TEXAS porches."

Sam told Tweed, "See? She might be trainable."

Tweed dismissed the idea. "Two days isn't long enough to retrain a Virginia lady."

She inquired in a hoity-toity manner, "Isn't Virginia said in caps?"

Both men replied at once, "No." Then they crossed glances and shared a slight, asinine smile and their eyelids almost closed over their humor.

She walked to the end of the porch to look around. "The lake is here! I saw a pond as we came in, but I didn't realize it was so close to the house. All the trees," she explained, looking up into the oak, hackberry and pecan trees that crowded the house.

Sam explained, "That lake's for fires. Fires and ducks. The ducks keep the water weeds under control. When you swim, don't put your bare feet on the bottom. It's—muddy."

"Is that a diving platform?"

"Yep. Can you dive?"

She moved in such a way that they knew she would brag. "I'm the best belly flopper you've ever witnessed."

Sam laughed, but Tweed put in very seriously, "We swim naked."

She tilted her head back, raised her eyebrows and opened her mouth as she said a slow, "Oh." Then she brightened and lowered her chin with decision. "I'll close my eyes!"

Sam grinned at her; then he looked at her heels. "I love to hear a woman walking in heels. It's been a long, long time since such a pretty lady was here. But do you have any stout shoes? Any boots? I wonder if you could wear Ethel's."

"What size does she—"

Rather quickly, Tweed told her, "Ethel was Sam's wife."

She heard the "was" and waited.

Sam explained, "She was about your size. She was a pretty little lady, just like you. But her hair was a dark brown and her eyes were blue. I still miss her something awful."

Connie said, "Aw." But she didn't know what else to say to such a man.

Tweed's voice was gentle. "We could try the boots."

Sam said, "Some of her things are in the room we fixed up for Connie. Go see what's there. I didn't think a Virginia lady would have the things to wear that she might need around here."

Tweed lifted Connie's overnight bag and opened the porch screen door, holding it until she went inside. He told her, "The stairs're on the right, just around the corner."

She was looking around. "The pictures!"

Sam put in, "You'll have to notice they're all TEXAS scenes?"

Her eyes twinkled. "Yep."

But Tweed stopped Sam by asking, "How about the house tour tonight? She can see the computer then, too. We need to get her outside while it's light. You might make snide comments if I try to show her the ranch in the dark."

"I probably would."

She added, "Me, too."

Tweed shook his head to chide their sassiness. He escorted her across to the stairs, up them, and to a room at the back of the house, overlooking the lake. It was a wonderful, long view. She stood by the windows, looking out. "Ethel couldn't have found a lovelier place in heaven."

"See? You're adjusting."

"I just said it was pretty."

"You said it was heaven. Better than heaven. That's TEXAS thinking."

She put a hand to her forehead.

He frowned. "Are you all right? Would you like to rest for a while?"

She laughed. "I was being dramatic."

He nodded. "That's another trait. All TEXANS are dramatic. That's because they are so isolated and when they get the chance to talk, it goes to their heads and they show off something fierce."

"Okay, okay. Where are Ethel's boots?"

"Let's try the closet."

"How clever to keep shoes in the closet."

"TEXANS usually just put them by the bed, toes pointed out for a quick escape."

"Escape?"

"Wrong bed?" From the closet, he looked at her in innocent questioning.

"I would never have dreamed TEXANS could be philanderers."

"We do try." He lifted out a pair of the fanciest boots ever made. The horses on them were in colors of leather, and the flowers were also. They were something. The soles were hardly discolored. They'd barely been worn.

Tweed indicated she was to sit on the chair by the bed. He knelt down and slipped off her shoe. "Don't mind about your skirt. I wouldn't look." He looked. "I might peek, but I wouldn't stare."

"What would you expect to see?"

"Lace? Not too many of the guys I run into wear lace. A man gets haunted by the need—" he hesitated deliberately before he lifted his earnest gaze to hers and finished "—to see something feminine." And he grinned wickedly. "Brace your leg."

She did that, and the boot slid on quite easily. "Does your mother know you speak to ladies in this manner?"

He removed her other shoe. "God only knows who my mama was. Didn't I mention that she abandoned me at birth?"

"Well, *somebody* ought to be paying attention."

"You could monitor me. I probably have some rough edges." His tone indicated that would be a very minor thing. "Brace for it."

"What?"

"The boot!" He looked at her in innocent surprise.

She did that, and the other boot slid on easily. She stood up and walked, testing the fit. "It surprises me that you speak to me as you do...when you know what I was put through by...those men."

"That was them. This is me. I'm couth."

His replies were always so honest that she was startled by her response. She closed her lips on her laugh, but the sound was there in her throat, and her mouth betrayed the humor that danced in her eyes.

He raised his eyebrows over her smothered mirth. "I'm supposed to *demonstrate* couth to you?" He acted indignant that she should question that talent in him.

"I just think you have a very clever and soothing tongue."

"Yeah." He was smug, his eyelashes hiding his hot eyes. "I'll show you how clever my tongue can be. How are the boots?"

"I believe I need some thick socks. Hose won't do it."

"Don't tell Sam that Ethel's feet were bigger than yours."

"These boots are hardly worn. Maybe they were far too large, and Ethel couldn't keep them on *to* walk in them."

He added: "Or maybe killingly small?"

"Whichever. With thick socks, I can handle this."

They both looked at his feet. His socks would be too big for her.

He shifted his feet and alibied, "I would'a been taller if so much of me hadn't been turned under." He had large feet.

They both laughed. Then she suggested, "Maybe Sam's socks would do it?"

"I'll check it out. Wait here. Don't move."

"Why not?"

"I want to escort you downstairs."

She answered readily enough, "All right."

So he explained more clearly. "I have dibs on your company for these whole two days. Nobody else can touch you."

"That could confine you rather severely."

"There's no other woman around. I like being around you. I have priority."

"This was discussed." It was a statement. Her gaze was on his face.

Quite blandly, he responded with a nod. "I threatened their very lives. But you have to do your share and wait for me and watch for me. I can't have one of them sneaking you off and showing you the pigs or taking you out skinny-dipping, for Pete's sake."

Snippily, she inquired, "And why would I do anything for Pete?"

"Fortunately, on this place, there is no single person named Pete. Stay." He put his hand out toward her and commanded that.

"I'm hardly a dog."

He grinned at her. "No match at all. Don't move."

But she did. She took off her panty hose.

He was back in a minute and tapped on the closed door as he opened it.

She was just completing her elaborate stance in a half run, her arms out, teetering.

He regarded her with patience. "I didn't say freeze, I said stay, and that's different."

"Oh." She stood back on the floor in sweet obedience.

"Sam could'a been right, although he rarely is. You just might be trainable."

"Bark, bark, bark."

He sighed and shook his head. "Sit."

She did choose a chair.

He removed the boots, rolled on the socks and put the boots back on.

She stood, walked around, strutted, clomped and declared, "They're great!"

He said softly, "So are you."

# Five

No one was anywhere around when Tweed took Connie downstairs, preceding her as a gentleman does to protect a lady from tumbling on stairs. They went out onto the porch. There was no sound. Well, the breeze was rustling the leaves in a nice, soft way. Some calf was bawling at a distance. There were chatting birds. But no metal was clanking or motor insisting on something, nor was there any abrasive sound.

Tweed was silent, letting her soak that in.

She frowned slightly and said, "It's very still."

With her words, he then knew that she was listening as she'd listened in that hollow where she'd been the only one alive anywhere around. How was he to handle that? His mind ran at light speed and he came up with, "Listen to the ducks."

She almost smiled, but her face was pale.

He took her arm and said, "I'll drive so you can look around."

She had looked around. Ever since she first came to TEXAS, she'd looked around. It was an empty land. This would be a test, to look at it all and see it all again, as it had been, there in the hollow.

In the car, she could turn her head away and close her eyes. She could be safe in the car with Tweed. She could just let his voice soothe her as it had since she'd first heard him call out. As much as she'd wanted another human, she had resisted running and flinging herself at him because she had no idea if he was one of the others who'd been there.

A great greyhound came silently up the steps and onto the porch. She didn't move. But the dog didn't bare his teeth or snarl. He was a gentleman. Tweed put his hands on the dog, petting him a little rougher than Connie thought he should handle such a large dog. Then Tweed pulled its face up so they looked eye to eye, and said, "Hello, boy."

The dog whipped its tail back and forth and smiled, its front feet dancing.

Tweed laughed and said, "He wants me to pick him up like I did three years ago when he was a puppy. No way, boy, settle down."

And the dog did.

Tweed said, "This is Finnigan. He's an all-round dog—" Tweed gestured "—house, barn, horse, cattle, guard, you name it. He knows over 150 words, so watch how you talk."

"Finnigan? Why... Finnigan?"

"An Irish dog should have an Irish name."

"I suppose."

Then Tweed told Connie, "Give me your hand. Now, Finnigan, this is Connie. You're to guard her and keep her safe. Understand?" Tweed was aware Connie's hand was cold, and she was reluctant to be so close to the hound. Had there been a big, mean dog in the hollow?

He asked, "Have you met a dog as big as Finnigan... lately?"

She shook her head, but then she realized what he was asking. "No. I was bitten as a child by a strange dog. I'm not partial to them."

"You'll love Finnigan."

She wasn't convinced.

Tweed said to the dog, "She's family. You're to care for her. Understand? Shake hands."

The dog listened to Tweed as he watched Connie very seriously. Then the dog shifted somewhat and lifted his right paw.

Tweed instructed the silent woman, "Shake hands with him. That seals the command."

Shake hands with that monster? She glanced at Tweed, who was serious. The dog waited patiently. Connie leaned over and shook the paw.

Finnigan broke from his position and walked around a little, with his nose to the porch. His grin was really wide.

Tweed said, "He thinks it's funny that you didn't want to touch him. He's macho and loves startling people. He does it deliberately."

Finnigan had sat back down and was grinning ear to ear with his tongue hanging out... and his teeth in evidence.

"You ought to see him snarl with all his teeth showing and his lips drawn back. The sounds he makes are scary."

"I'd rather not."

"He's also a snake dog. So he's going along, but I'll drive."

"All right."

He took her elbow and led her down the stairs to the Jag. "I meant that I won't let Finnigan drive. I'll drive."

"Finnigan . . . drives?"

Tweed put her into the car as he explained, "He thinks he can drive, but he can't see over the steering wheel and reach the pedals at the same time." He went around the car and let Finnigan into the car and onto the back seat. He said to the dog, "Don't drool over on the front seat. Try to be a gentleman."

"Is this all a new-boy joke?"

"No, ma'am. I'm just stating the facts." He took off his Stetson and put it on the back seat, saying to Finnigan, "Don't sit on it."

The dog gave a soft sound in response.

She asked, "Do you move your hands to get the correct sound replies from the dog?"

He was astonished. "He hears, and he replies or acknowledges...or disagrees. Try never to argue with Finnigan. He never lets up. He's just like a wom— Uhhh. He's relentless."

She laughed. Out loud!

That's probably when Tweed fell in love with her.

They sat, grinning, their eyes sparkling with their humor, watching each other for a minute or two. Then he said, "Brace yourself, you're about to see the most beautiful part of beautiful, beautiful TEXAS. Did you know there's a song about that?" And as they started out, he sang every endless four-lined verse of that four-versed, over-coated, face-flinching song.

When it was finished, Tweed assured her, "You can be a TEXAN and not sing that."

"Why would I want to be a Texan?"

"You flubbed it again."

She corrected, "A TEXAN."

"That's better. One never knows how one's life has been charted. One goes along and learns where one is supposed to light, and why."

"I'm to become a drifter?"

"You might not be a Virginian."

She looked off out the window. It seemed that he drove forever. The "roads" were two-wheel path-of-least-resistance tracks.

He stopped the car and emerged, leaving the door open. He buckled on a gun belt and took the gun out and checked it.

"Why do you have a gun?"

"A guy never knows what he might come up on. You never know for certain."

She couldn't argue with that.

He showed her cattle that looked back at them with curiosity. Some stood back under the short mesquite trees and watched. Some came to the barbed-wire fence, and they were e-nor-mous. There were busy flies in the fur on the backs of the cattle.

Finnigan sat and watched.

"I thought you said he was a cattle dog."

"He is. Do you want him to move that herd?"

"No. But shouldn't they be back from the fence?"

"No. That side's their territory—for now."

They got back into the car, and he took her to see a canyon. They stopped and exited the car. Finnigan got out, too, to look around, before he ranged off and about. The two humans had only to walk a short distance. Tweed was being careful of her stamina. He told her, "This is why you needed the boots. Sometimes rattlesnakes resent people coming along and startling them."

"Snakes." She tested the word.

He gestured with a logical hand and admitted, "Even Eden had snakes."

The canyon wasn't the Grand Canyon. It was a miniature and it was, indeed, lovely. It went down about thirty feet, and the stream below was clear and idyllic as it ate gently at the base of the drop. The colors were subtle and thrilled the eye with the variance. Twisted by the wind, the little scrub cedars clung bravely here and there. And along the edge were the hardy, deep-rooted, irritating mesquites.

Tweed explained, "The leaves of mesquite trees aren't thick enough for much shade. And the scrawny trees aren't tall enough to climb to get away from something really nasty. They have deep roots that suck up the ground water, and they crowd out trees we'd prefer. They're thorny and nasty and the wood is sparse and tough and twisted. It isn't a tree to encourage."

Then gesturing at the tiny canyon, Tweed told her, "Somebody, some long time ago, could have prevented this gully with just a series of rock piles to slow the water wash. But look at the soil layers. Isn't that pretty?"

She looked, but she added, "Even burned-out buildings can be beautiful if you don't think of the destruction. If you look at something in contrast or symmetry, anything is beautiful."

He shook his head. "Not a dead cow with the buzzards at it." Then he bit his tongue because he'd spoken of death.

She demurred, "Even that."

He wondered what she would say if he questioned the beauty of her dead uncle. Or the beauty of her own bruises. Then he looked at her perfect face and remembered the marvelous colors of the bruises—but the beauty was as the bruises had healed.

He said, "Another time, when it hasn't rained northwest of here and you're used to walking in boots and you have on denim, we'll go down and explore. It's really beautiful."

"When it hasn't rained northwest?"

"That's when we get gully washers under a sunny sky. Walk along something like that, down there, and all of a sudden there comes a wall of water rushing down on you with the roar of a freight train. The water comes from far, far away. You gotta be careful of gulleys."

"It looks—isolated."

"It is."

"I'm glad you're here."

She had been terrified to be alone in the hollow. He replied, "I'm glad, too. It's special to show somebody the beauties you yourself enjoy. This is the place."

"What place?"

"I had to find it. All of my life I have been in the wrong place. I felt it. I had to hunt for this one. I've finally realized that I want to be here."

She looked into his clear blue eyes and saw how serious he was. He'd had no roots. He'd found himself a place. "I'm glad your mother left you there and didn't harm you."

"She put me in a trash bin."

"But you were found."

"I'm glad of that... now."

"You haven't appreciated living?"

"No. Not until just lately. I had no purpose. No roots. I didn't belong anywhere." He started back, but then he remembered to turn to see if she was ready. She followed, but she realized he wasn't used to being with a woman, and it was different for him to consider her opinion. But he shared his ideas with her and welcomed hers.

As they strolled the short distance, he confided, "One of the strange things I've learned is that there are people everywhere who aren't sure they should be where they are. It must be the gene that made people move here from around the world. They're all looking." As he opened the car door for her, he gave her a slight smile. "They're probably not from this planet and don't realize their 'place' isn't on this one."

She sat on the seat to swing her legs into the car as she replied, "So those are the people who are urging that we explore space? They want to go home."

"Exactly." He closed her door and walked around the car. Then he whistled for Finnigan and indicated the dog should get into the back seat. That done, Tweed again put his Stetson onto the back seat and slid into the driver's seat. "I've got a place for us to have lunch. I'll tell you when to close your eyes."

So as he drove, she looked around more avidly, moving her head, stretching up to see better.

He accused, "You're trying to get a glimpse of something different so when I tell you to close your eyes, you'll already know and won't be curious."

Her grin confirmed that.

It wasn't long before he slowed and said, "Okay. Close your eyes." Then he reached his right hand over and cupped that hand, thumb down, over her eyes. "Got them closed?"

She said a sassy, "Well, it doesn't really matter, does it?"

"You peeked! You peeked or you wouldn't have known I don't trust you."

He drove one-handed, looking from the road to her, until he had slowly swung the car to the left and stopped.

He said, "Okay, you cheat, you can look now."

She looked at him and shared their humor. She looked ahead and there were more of the mesquite trees. Then she looked aside and saw it.

It was a big, old oak tree, and built to one side of it was a grand staircase to a porch that was constructed in the middle of the tree. There was a porch rather than a deck. It was one level and had an ornate railing around it. It was beautiful. Incongruous. Amazing.

She exclaimed with delight.

All three got out. As usual, Tweed looked around. Outside, he never quit looking. The dog roamed off to check out the area. Tweed reset his Stetson and went to the car trunk to get the picnic paraphernalia. And Connie went to the bottom of the wide, slightly curved stair. It had been built that way to avoid a large limb. She stood there at the bottom of those stairs, looking around. "What an elegant place."

"Ethel used to give tea parties here. She did a great job of it, Sam says. And after formal dinners at the house, they'd come out here in their fine clothes and have after-dinner drinks. An orchestra would play for them as they talked and gossiped."

"What a wonderful imagination to have contrived this perfect spot. How unique!"

"Ethel apparently was."

"You never knew her."

"No. And I regret it. I will always wonder what she would have done about . . . me."

"Done about you?"

"She was such an innovator, and I was so at a loss, that I wonder what she would have suggested for me. She was a solver. She bought the computer. Sam's only now getting around to finding out how it works."

They mounted the stairs to the porch. There were several small tables. Like the ice-cream-parlor chairs, the tables were metal. They had no dust on them. The floor had been swept as had the stairs. Someone had come and tidied the place for their casual picnic. Had it been Tweed?

He carried two baskets. He put them on one table. He opened the first basket and took out some Handi Wipes to clean their hands. He gave his hands a swipe, but she was more diligent, having shaken the dog's paw.

Tweed removed a bottle of wine and the glasses which had been cushioned in heavy linen napkins. He set them aside. He took out an ecru cloth that was edged with handmade lace.

Connie took it from him and put it on another table. He handed her napkins, sterling flatware, plates that were delicately painted and stemmed glasses. He poured cold water into one glass and chilled wine into the second one for each of them.

He opened the other basket and removed finger sandwiches that were elegantly done, cucumber and watercress, white chicken bits with parsley, shaved ham and cheese. Then he put out two thick, complicated sandwiches on his own plate. He gave her a smug glance. She shook her head chidingly, but she grinned.

He put an exquisite bowl filled with fruit in the middle of the table. He opened another bottle of dessert wine, to breathe, and set it on the other table.

He held her chair for her and said, "Don't for a minute think I'm this elegant. This is all Jake. He gave me those sandwiches because he knew I'd starve on those tiny things he's fixed for you. If I fainted from hunger, you'd probably have had to give me mouth-to-mouth to revive me, and he never does anything that might help me with a woman. He knows I'm not good enough for you, so you can see he's trying to defend you from me." Tweed's expression was tolerant and without the least indication of being inferior.

She looked off and then looked down as she smiled and bit her lower lip to keep from laughing.

The food was delicious. Who would ever believe that Jake could be so delicate as a chef? The nuances of flavor were so subtle that her palate was delighted.

"What wine is this?" she asked.

"I don't know. It isn't beer, that's about all the information I can give you."

"You prefer beer?"

"Yeah. But I can tolerate this stuff. It isn't bad." He licked his lips, and the humor danced in his eyes.

"You chose the wine."

"Jake did."

She turned the bottle in the wine holder and said, "Tell me the name."

He replied, "I wanted champagne, but he said that some ladies get looped on champagne and lose their heads. I said, 'So?' And he put this stuff in the basket. I told you. He's protecting you from me."

"Are you a violent man?"

"No. I know that's crass, so I try the candy's-dandy-but-likker's-quicker route."

"You said you were . . . couth."

"Oh, I am." Then he gently whirled the wine in his glass and sniffed it before he took a token sip.

She watched that with lowered eyelids and a quirk of her lips.

He said, "It has a nice bouquet. Chrysanthemums, right?"

She had to laugh.

Their lunch was excellent, their conversation flirting and light, and their unique place was perfect.

Tweed, being couth, emptied the fruit out onto that lovely cloth and filled the fragile bowl with water to take down to Finnigan.

The dog wasn't allowed on the stairs, much less on the contrived gallery. He didn't mind. He'd investigated it any number of unsupervised times. If they thought he wasn't supposed to be on it, then that was all right with him.

The pair sat and talked and talked and talked. And laughed. Ah, what humor he had. She listened and watched and rebutted the fantastic facts he supplied. She sassed and gestured and was quite animated.

He noted all that with hooded, amused eyes as he saw the change in her. She was going to be all right.

She would make it. Time would soften the edges of that terrible exerience for her.

Not only the experience of the multiple assault, but seeing her uncle beaten so badly. The uncle must have lived long enough to get the rifle and kill her attackers. She wasn't strong enough to have done that herself. And her uncle must have cut them. Think of his revenge on them. He would have died in triumph.

Or had it been she?

He watched her as she ate so nicely, as she gently blotted her lips on the cloth napkin, as she replied to his outrageous statements, and he knew that he had no idea of her strengths. He could find no weaknesses.

She was confident out there in the midst of nowhere with a man she really knew nothing about. No. She'd asked Betty Lou. Not Sanford. She'd asked another woman. She was cautious.

Had that Betty Lou told Connie that he was harmless? Tweed was offended. That put the burden of correct behavior on his shoulders. On his conscience.

He inquired, "Since you know I was raised by a lot of different people, haphazardly, why are you out here in the wilds of TEXAS with me?"

"I'm not sure."

"Are you a reckless woman?"

"I hadn't ever thought so." She was serious then. Her expression was sober and interested. She wasn't flirting or teasing, but she wasn't at all uncertain. She was calm.

He would have done anything to have gone on asking her questions about the assault and, as badly beaten as her uncle was, how had he gotten the rifle?

He said, "I must say that your momma sure did teach you nice-lady manners. You make eating into an art."

"There's no marketable value in eating nicely. That's why I have a master's in business."

"I haven't had much education."

"You mean formal education. I've met few men smarter than you."

"You know nothing about me at all."

"I know more about you than you realize."

"How could that be? You haven't been conscious through most of our acquaintance."

"I remember how you acted…when…we…met."

"I didn't know you'd been hurt. Not at first."

Her eyes went out of focus. It was too soon. Her lips paled and she turned her head to look blankly off into the distance. She shivered.

He went to her and took her from her chair. He went back to his chair and held her on his lap. "I'm sorry, Connie. Do you need to cry or talk?"

She shook her head. But she shivered again.

He stood up and carried her across the contrived porch and down the grand staircase. He carried her to the car and set her on her feet before he opened the car door. "I'll take you back to the house, and I'll come back for the rest of the stuff."

"No. I'll be all right in the car. I can wait."

She'd be enclosed. Protected. It was like a capsule. Like the plane. The car. A house.

He put her into the car and whistled for Finnigan. He didn't put the dog into the car, but he said, "Guard," so that Connie could hear him tell that to the big gray dog.

Then Tweed went up the steps and gathered the picnic things. He corked the dessert wine and put it into the basket. He put what the birds would eat out on the ground below, and he carried the rest back to the car's trunk.

That done, he opened the car door and allowed the dog to get in the back. Then he got in and looked at Connie. She was unconscious!

He was appalled. He reached in back and got a jacket and covered her.

She murmured and smiled a little, opening her eyes. "Sorry. I had no idea I was so sleepy. It must have been the wine."

Asleep? She'd only been asleep! His eyes watered and he had to swallow. "Settle down," he told her softly. "It's only a little way. Just about two blocks by the road. It's only about half a block from the house."

"Ummmm."

That sound lifted his hair. It was too much like the sounds she'd made in the hospital.

He drove very carefully.

When they got to the house, he slid out of the car and carefully closed the door. Dusty was near, and Tweed signaled him to come there, then to be quiet.

"Hold the door, go up the stairs and open the bedroom door at the back of the house."

"Is she all right?"

"Just tired. She needs a nap."

"What'd you do t'her?" Dusty frowned at Tweed.

"Nothing." He looked offended.

But Dusty was a little hostile. At the porch, Sam came out the door.

Dusty said, "She's out cold."

"What's the matter?"

"Tweed said she's sleepy."

"Yeah. Run along. I'll hold the door."

"If you need me—" Dusty didn't want to leave.

"We'll sure whistle. Go along, now."

So it was Sam on the porch who watched how gently Tweed removed the limp girl from the car, but he saw how her arms slid around his shoulders and how she smiled as she put her head between his head and shoulder.

Tweed carefully carried her up the steps and was on the porch when he saw the door was being held by Sam. He nodded at Sam and went on inside to wait until the older man softly closed the door, then went ahead, across the entrance hall and up the stairs.

He stood in the bedroom doorway as Tweed laid Connie on the big, soft bed. He removed her boots but left the socks on her. He loosened her belt but left her clothes on. Then he covered her with a remarkable, handmade patchwork quilt that was named the Star of Bethlehem.

Tweed stood and looked at her as he chewed his lip; then he turned toward the door and appeared surprised to see Sam still there. He nodded again, followed Sam from the room and carefully closed the door.

In the hall, Tweed whispered, "I need to call Sanford."

"What happened?"

"We were just talking. She mentioned our meeting, and I said that I hadn't known then that she'd been hurt. Just those words must have brought it all back to her. Her eyes went out of focus and she shivered. I carried her down to the car. She feels safe in confined places. She said I could bring back the luncheon stuff. When I brought it to the car, I thought she was unconscious, but she was asleep. She roused and spoke to me.''

"I guess we got her out here too soon."

"No." Tweed was sure. "She has enjoyed being here. It was just too much, too soon. After a nap, she'll be all right. But I don't believe we ought to show her the computer tonight. We might wait for another time and have her come out again. She's not as strong as she looks."

# Six

Neither man left the house in those next several hours. They paced. It wasn't long before they removed their boots, because the floors were mostly bare and they'd become aware of their clinking steps.

Tweed finally went to the kitchen and helped Jake with supper. He told the cook, "You're a fine chef, that's what she said. She said you were a magician. I wish you coulda seen her expression when she ate the dainties you made for her."

"You shoulda taken the camcorder. I coulda shown it at my next interview."

"You leaving again?" Jake was always threatening to quit.

"Not right away." Jake looked down as he raised his eyebrows. "I'm just looking ahead."

Tweed coaxed, "For Connie's sake, stay through her visit."

"I might."

Those debates and adjustments had become a fine art.

Jake asked with narrowed eyes, "You didn't try to jump her, did you?"

"Aw, for crying out loud, I got more finesse than that."

"She's a lady."

"I know that."

"She's had a bad time."

"Do you know that when I found her, she'd had to put on some of their clothes? Do you realize what that must have cost her?"

After a silence, Tweed heard Jake sniffle. Tweed looked up as Jake wiped his nose on his shoulder.

Tweed reached into his back pocket, brought out a pristine handkerchief and handed it to Jake. Tweed had carried that handkerchief in case Connie might have needed one. She might have gotten a dust speck in her eye or something, and he'd wanted a really clean handkerchief.

He'd been prepared. Like Gregory? No. Tweed rejected that he could be anything like Gregory. He'd just wanted not to gross her out if she'd needed a handkerchief when she was with him.

Tweed watched as Jake blew his nose like a freight train coming to the junction. How could such a crude man be such a fine cook? Automatically, Tweed said, "Wash your hands."

Sam had told Tweed that was all Ethel had ever said to Jake.

After two hours, and it was getting on past three o'clock, Tweed asked Sam, "Do you suppose we ought to check on her?"

"Sanford said to leave her sleep."

"But she ought to be awake in the daylight hours and not up and prowling at night."

"Sanford says she has a couple of sleeping pills."

But when it was almost four o'clock, it was Sam who began to fret. He said, "Maybe you ought to go up and take a peek at her. Knock first. If she's still asleep by four, Sanford said to stimulate her."

"Just what do you suppose he had in mind?"

Sam was patient. "Nothing like what just flashed through yours, you tomcat. You got to be subtle. You pat her cheek or tickle the bottom...of her foot. Fooled you there, didn't I?"

"No, I'm used to you."

So as the clock ticked to four, Jake came in with his rolled-up denim shirtsleeves and his tea-towel apron and said he had a Tea ready.

Sam and Tweed exchanged a stunned glance. A Tea? Capitalized?

"You've never made us a Tea before this, how'd you know how?"

"I got untapped talents."

And Sam agreed, "You are a skilled cook. Skilled and innovative."

Jake tasted the word "innovative" and nodded.

So Tweed went upstairs to waken the sleeping beauty. He tapped on her door, and his back prickled with a touch of alarm when she didn't reply. He opened the door gently, and she was sleeping soundly.

He went into her room, leaving the door open, and walked stocking footed over to the bed, where he filled his parched soul with the sight of her. Maybe what was affecting him was more than just plain love. It could be serious.

# NO COST! NO OBLIGATION TO BUY!
# NO PURCHASE NECESSARY!

## PLAY "LUCKY 7"
## AND GET AS MANY AS FIVE FREE GIFTS.

# HOW TO PLAY:

1. With a coin, carefully scratch off the silver box at the right. This makes you eligible to receive two or more free books, and possibly another gift, depending on what is revealed beneath the scratch-off area.

2. Send back this card and you'll receive brand-new Silhouette Desire® novels. These books have a cover price of $2.99 each, but they are yours to keep absolutely free.

3. There's no catch. You're under no obligation to buy anything. We charge nothing—ZERO—for your first shipment. And you don't have to make any minimum number of purchases—not even one!

4. The fact is thousands of readers enjoy receiving books by mail from the Silhouette Reader Service™ months before they're available in stores. They like the convenience of home delivery and they love our discount prices!

5. We hope that after receiving your free books you'll want to remain a subscriber. But the choice is yours—to continue or cancel, anytime at all! So why not take us up on our invitation, with no risk of any kind. You'll be glad you did!

*This lovely Victorian pewter-finish miniature is perfect for displaying a treasured photograph. And it's yours FREE as added thanks for giving our Reader Service a try!*

**PLAY "LUCKY 7"**

**Just scratch off the silver box with a coin.
Then check below to see which gifts you get.**

**YES!** I have scratched off the silver box. Please send me all the gifts for which I qualify. I understand I am under no obligation to purchase any books, as explained on the back and on the opposite page.

326 CIS AK95
(C-SIL-D-11/93)

NAME

ADDRESS                                                      APT.

CITY                          PROVINCE          POSTAL CODE

| | | | |
|---|---|---|---|
| 7 | 7 | 7 | **WORTH FOUR FREE BOOKS PLUS A FREE VICTORIAN PICTURE FRAME** |
| 🍒 | 🍒 | 🍒 | **WORTH THREE FREE BOOKS PLUS A FREE VICTORIAN PICTURE FRAME** |
| ● | ● | ● | **WORTH THREE FREE BOOKS** |
| 🔔 | 🔔 | 🍒 | **WORTH TWO FREE BOOKS** |

DETACH AND MAIL CARD TODAY

# THE SILHOUETTE READER SERVICE™: HERE'S HOW IT WORKS

Accepting free books places you under no obligation to buy anything. You may keep the books and gift and return the shipping statement marked "cancel." If you do not cancel, about a month later we will send you 6 additional novels, and bill you just $2.49 each plus 25¢ delivery and GST.* That's the complete price and—compared to cover prices of $2.99 each—quite a bargain! You may cancel at any time, but if you choose to continue, every month we'll send you 6 more books, which you may either purchase at the discount price ... or return at our expense and cancel your subscription.

*Terms and prices subject to change without notice.
 Canadian residents will be charged applicable provincial taxes and GST.

0195619199-L2A5X3-BR01

SILHOUETTE READER SERVICE
PO BOX 609
FORT ERIE ON L2A 9Z9

MAIL ⟩ POSTE

Canada Post Corporation / Société canadienne des postes

Postage paid     Port payé
if mailed in Canada   si posté au Canada

Business     Réponse
Reply        d'affaires

0195619199     01

He asked softly, "Are you a night person?"

She yawned and stretched her arms up and out from under the remarkable quilt. He watched as if he'd never realized a woman could do either. He sat carefully on her bed with one knee near her blanketed hip. He put his elbow on that knee and propped his chin on his hand. He watched her open her eyes, and her smile was sleepy and affected him unduly.

"Are you a night person?" he inquired for a second time.

"What time is it?"

"Just at four."

"This bed is a cloud."

He frowned. "Nobody told me that. How come you got a good bed? Mine's lumpy, and I think the dogs slept on it before I came here."

She contemplated him with amused tolerance.

He found amused tolerance was an aphrodisiac. "Are you okay?"

"I think it was the wine."

He didn't contradict her. He "saw" her again as he had in the deserted hollow that first time. She'd been strung out. This was probably the first natural sleep she'd had since then. "Did you sleep well?"

"It was wonderful. I love the curtains blowing in the breeze."

"Were you warm enough?"

She smiled past him and said, "Have I been a poor guest, sleeping all afternoon?"

Tweed replied, "No."

From the door, Sam also said, "No."

Without turning, Tweed said, "I thought I was going to have to kiss her and remove the bite of poisoned apple from her lips."

And from in back of Sam, Jake said snidely, "Been reading fairy tales?"

Tweed chuckled, still watching Connie.

Jake said, "I brought enough for us all."

And it was then that Tweed turned his head and saw that Sam and Jake had brought the formal Tea to her. They were going to spoil her rotten. He looked at her face and saw that she was surprised.

"Tea? How thoughtful."

Jake told her sorrowfully, "The biscuits aren't as they should be. But the cinnamon and sugar will make them tolerable."

Sam and Jake moved a round table over near the bed, and Tweed got a sweater for Connie as a bed jacket. She was still in her dress, but after sleeping under the quilt she would be cool if she sat up without something around her shoulders.

She allowed them to rearrange her pillows, and she exclaimed over the tray. She sympathized to Jake about the biscuits not being perfect until she tasted one. Then she met Jake's smug eyes, and she shook her head at him chidingly. She broke the English biscuit and the texture was exactly right. She said to Jake, "You knew it was perfect."

"Well, I've made better."

"I don't see how."

He tilted his head and looked down to hide the pride in his eyes, and he licked neatly at his smile.

The three men arranged their own seating. Jake was on a window seat so that he could keep track of how much they really enjoyed the Tea. Sam gingerly sat on a needlepointed ladies' chair by the table, and Tweed was back on the bed facing Connie.

They competed for her amusement with some subtlety.

Sam said, "You ought not sit on the bed. You'll tilt her tray."

"I have to be close to give her mouth-to-mouth if she chokes on that hardtack Jake's insisting we eat."

"Bosh!" Connie snubbed Tweed, but she grinned. She told Jake, "How envious he is of your cooking. He must be a peanut-butter man."

Jake nodded and licked his lips some more. "And he reads fairy tales."

"Does he?" She looked at Tweed, who met her glance and winked.

She told Jake, "I was never allowed to read fairy tales at home. My parents said they were wicked and untrue. That parents didn't actually take their little children into the deep woods and leave them there. And that any mother would probably object to a daughter bringing a frog home and taking it to bed."

Tweed turned to Jake. "See?"

What that actually meant no one ever discovered, because that one word set up lines that argued so heatedly that they ended up deciding what to do about the national debt!

Sam asked, "How'd we get to this?"

Tweed replied, "I wasn't even involved."

Jake said, "You were, too! You said—"

It all started all over, and the four were late for supper.

The people on the place all ate together in a long, screened room off the kitchen. Since they had to eat on time, supper was fried ham, soufflés perfectly done, hash-brown potatoes with a fruit salad and hot, crispy rolls toasted by an agitated Jake. It was the

other three who set the table and explained to the
hands what had happened.

The men teased Jake-the-Clock, who protested, "I
had no idea it was so late!"

Connie asked, "But wasn't it fun?"

"Yes," agreed the flustered Jake, "but I didn't get
the meat marinated."

She soothed, "We'll have it tomorrow."

He said hollowly, "We have fillet of sole tomorrow."

"I'll stay an extra day."

The other men cheered. Even Jake seemed pleased.

But as he served the table with Freddy to help, Jake
agitated, "We'll have to have something else for
breakfast if you stay another day. I can't feed you
hash-brown potatoes and grits with your bacon and
eggs."

"Why not?"

He was shocked. "You're a lady."

"I'll try to remember that."

It was Dusty who asked, "Why did Jake forget to
fix supper?"

The table conversation had been rather sparse until
then. But the four told of their conversation and how
it had gotten clear off base and out of hand.

But hearing what they'd talked about only made the
others at the table give their own opinions. The exchange was loud and there was laughter and argu-
ments and hands slapped down on the table to make
a point.

Sam listened to the bedlam and smiled.

But he realized that it was Tweed who controlled
and guided the speakers. It was he who asked an
opinion from one of the men who wasn't a blusterer.

It was Tweed who saw that those arguing didn't get angry. Again, Sam wondered about the man, Salty, who had so influenced this wayfarer who'd come to him.

And Sam saw how Connie listened . . . to Tweed.

She watched him, she glanced at him to see his reactions, but while she was exquisitely aware of Tweed, she did listen to them all.

She was charming. She didn't flirt or show off or strive to garner notice, but all the men who spoke vied for her attention. They were clever to make her laugh. And when they won her laughter, it was like an olive-leaf crown of victory.

So it shouldn't have been a surprise, some time after they'd finally left, that some of the men came back and serenaded Connie. They came to the porch with guitars and began to strum them.

Tweed went out on the porch and said, "I hate to tell you this, but she's around in back."

"We know. Dusty told us. But we thought we'd be polite and pretend we was serenading the whole bunch."

Tweed nodded seriously and advised, "Go around the back, like the tomcats you are, and yowl at her. She's a-bed. But don't you guys carry on too long, she's a little tired."

"Three songs?"

"That'll be just about right."

While Tweed thought nothing at all about his interference and directions, Sam noted it all. So, Tweed was really very territorial. Did Tweed realize that?

Well, sure. Tweed then walked through the door, up the stairs, and tapped on Connie's door. He then paused briefly and opened the door to the dark room. "You asleep?" he whispered.

Also whispering, she replied, "I'm not even in bed. How fast do you believe I could get to sleep? I'm so stimulated with all the talk that I'm sitting here thinking of all the rebuttals I didn't get in."

"You're an argumentative woman."

She whispered a shrugging, "Yeah."

Below her window, the music started.

"What's that?" she asked softly.

He crossed to where her voice was. He noted in passing that her bed's covering was turned back. His voice hushed, he told her, "The guys are serenading you. It's okay for you to sit in your window and admire them. If you want to acknowledge that you love the man singing, and you have a rose, you unlatch the screen and drop it down."

He'd found her sitting on the window seat that was even with the bottom of the windows. She was half turned away, looking down at the five men below. Tweed eased down beside her. Quietly he asked, "You warm enough?"

She nodded.

He was glad for the music because his breathing was rough and loud. He enclosed her without touching her. He put his hand on the windowsill in back of her, and said in her ear, "They're better than they used to be."

The voices were really pretty good. Their strumming was basic, but their voices were true. The songs were country-western, naturally, and like most people carried away by their music, they were almost impossible to understand.

She breathed the words, very aware of his nearness. "What are the lyrics?"

"Excruciatingly plaintive. A little like tomcats on a fence."

She smothered giggles.

After the third song, the musicians struck some chords, and then they began to walk away. Connie pulled back the curtain and called, "That was lovely. Thank you."

And the five said variations of "Good night."

She put the curtain back and turned to find herself not only discreetly enclosed but very close to Tweed. She sat absolutely still.

His breathing was audible. She heard him lick his lips and take a breath. His breath shivered. She had been a bit alarmed to find him so close, but the sound of his disciplined but shivery breath touched in her.

She leaned across that tiny distance and kissed him very gently.

His arms were instantly around her in controlled hunger. He drew in his breath raggedly through his nose because his mouth was glued to hers. He helped with the sweet kiss, but turned it into something else entirely.

When he finally lifted his mouth from hers, he said with earnest gentleness, "Don't be afraid of me."

Her breaths were uneven.

He kissed her face and found the tear. He remembered kissing tears on her face at the hospital. His heart was twisted. "Oh, Connie."

How could two words carry such anguish?

He began to release her, forcing his big hands to let her go. But she put her hand to the back of his head, and her mouth was sweet under his. As she finally broke the kiss, she said, "You're a special man."

It was gratitude. Hell. He moved back a little.
"Have you brushed your teeth?"

"Yes, sir."

"Then you ought to get into bed. It's really kinda
late for you. Do you need a sleeping pill? Where are
the pills?"

"Here, by the bed."

"You know better than to do that. With them so
handy, that way, you could overdose."

"Where would be a good place?"

"I'm just down the hall. That second door. I'll leave
the door open and if you wake up and can't get back
to sleep, come to me and I'll...give you the other pill."

"All right."

She turned on the light. She was in a cotton robe
that was almost like silk. Against the light, he could
see her form. She was obviously unaware that the light
revealed the silhouette of her body to him. She leaned
over, and he could see the sweet outline of her breast
as she reached for her purse. He couldn't breathe at
all.

She got the pills from her purse, shook one pill out
of the container, then capped the bottle and handed it
to him.

He was responsible for her.

If she came to him in the night and said she couldn't
sleep, would he lift his sheet and invite her into his
bed? Or would he have the fortitude to only give her
another pill?

He asked casually, "Want me to sleep with you? I'm
warm-blooded. I'd keep you toasty warm."

She scoffed.

"If you couldn't sleep, I could...entertain you."

She chuckled. "More serenading?"

Tweed thought of their black tomcat. "Yeah."

"Thank you, but I'll try it solo."

"I want you comfortable in this house. I hope you sleep like you did this afternoon, and without a pill."

"Thanks, Tweed.... Tweed, you were going to show me the coat!"

"I'll do that tomorrow."

"All right. Good night."

"G'night."

She didn't move to him, so he didn't feel he could kiss her again. He was awkward with her. When had Tweed Brown ever been awkward with a woman? When had a woman ever mattered so much?

He went to her opened door and looked back. "I'm just down there, second door. If you need me, I'd hear you holler."

"I'd do that."

"Well," he said. "G'night."

She smiled, standing there against the light on the bed table.

It was one of the times when a Tweed black mark was erased from Saint Peter's record book. Tweed was sure of that as he left her room and went down to his.

It took him a while to fall asleep. It was so still. He'd never before noticed how silent the night was out yonder. No traffic, no fire engines, no police cars, no loud voices or slamming doors. Nothing. The clock didn't even tick.

He went back in his mind to his first memory, that of being in a quarreling house where things had been thrown and where there had been shouted words with swearing.

He remembered finally getting to the Browns' and how resistant he'd been to everything by then. Who

could ever believe people could be kind and gentle?
Tweed had had a hard time understanding that could
happen to him. From Salty and Felicia, he'd learned
a lot, but it had been hard to understand that they
were really on his side.

And—just like that—it came to him that he'd survived the news that Carol Brown was married ... to
another man. Tweed had known, all along, that
someday it would happen. He would hear of it, like
now, after the fact and he would suffer.

He searched his heart and found that he and Carol
had never been suited. She was off in the world of
creativity, and he was in the practical world of eating
and sleeping. As magical as she'd been, he had never
aspired to actually claiming her. Had he, he would
have kept in touch so that she would have remembered him.

She was special, there was no question of that.
Ethereal. And she'd chosen a policeman? A policeman. Carol's husband was a policeman who wrote
horror books. Tweed frowned at the ceiling and
thought maybe he ought to check the guy out.

Of course, Salty wouldn't have allowed her to marry
someone unsuitable. What if he'd had no idea it was
happening? Salty had always been a hands-off man.
He'd directed the kids and channeled them, but he'd
been hands-off about it.

Hands-off? And Tweed remembered the lesson in
living that Salty had once given him in the barn.

He'd deserved it.

He'd been, what, fifteen? Close. Tweed had been so
foulmouthed and belligerent. Salty had been so sure
and so calm. He'd told Tweed what was expected of
him, and Tweed had said— Two words.

Salty had called him on that, and Tweed had become mutinous and rough mouthed.

Salty had watched him calmly; then he'd said, "You need a lesson. Stand there."

Hostile, Tweed felt he could handle Salty, and he'd stood as directed. He expected Salty to attack him. Other men had.

But Salty had gone over to the barn wall and undone a rope. He began to play out the rope without undue attention to Tweed.

Tweed looked up and saw a square, single panel of bars coming down onto the barn floor. It was clumsy and strong. The bars were almost eighteen inches apart; it could block only a large animal from leaving a stall.

Salty guided the parallel bar section over so that it rested against a stall opening. He locked it into place, went through the widely spaced bars and set a stool there. Then he turned to Tweed and said, "In life, there are rules that must be followed so that a man has self-discipline. This cage won't actually hold you if you choose to leave, but there are jails that will. Sit on that stool and consider how you want your life to go."

Tweed was speechless. He stood and watched as Salty turned away and left the barn.

No one was anywhere around. Tweed had the choice of obeying or of walking off. It was a sobering lesson. He walked slowly to the cage and hesitated. He went easily through the bars and looked around. Then he sat on the stool and considered his life.

The words Salty had spoken to him were simple and understandable.

Thoughtfully, Tweed had cleaned up the barn, exactly. And in that following time, he'd done everything he was supposed to do, exactly. He set himself to be the best mechanic Salty had ever seen, and he did it, exactly. And having done all that, and proven to himself that he could, he took off. But he'd taken Salty's tweed coat with him.

After a time, it had been one of Tweed's personal triumphs to buy the most expensive tweed coat he could find, and send it to Salty to replace the one he'd taken. It was sent with gratitude and respect.

Life's little triumphs. Only when he bought that coat had Tweed realized all that Salty had really taught him. It wasn't skills or cleaning barns, it was what it took to be a man.

Tweed wondered what he could have been if Salty had had charge of him from the beginning? After his mother had thrown him into a trash bin, what if it had been Salty who had found him then?

And Tweed really considered what his mother must have been. Not a druggie. He'd been a healthy kid. Had she been a teenager who was terrified? Some helpless victim like Connie had been? Or a young girl who hadn't the means or the support to be cared about?

He pitied his mother and wondered what had happened to her. Poor woman. But she'd carried him. She'd given him this remarkable life. And in his heart, he thanked her.

It was only then that Tweed really looked at himself as a man. He considered himself and his conduct, and he knew that he was a good man. Like Connie said, he *was* a good man.

He smiled at the dark ceiling of his room and stretched his healthy body; then he turned over and went to sleep.

He wakened at six the next morning, as he'd trained himself to do. He smiled at the day and anticipated being busy. Then he remembered that Connie was down the hall. Was she awake? Naw. She'd probably sleep until noon.

After his shower, he dressed in jeans, a shirt and boots and stopped at her open door. She wasn't there. The sleeping pill was on the table by her bed. As he went downstairs, he lifted his nose to the aroma of baking bread.

Jake probably never slept. He was baking bread, and the smell would allow a man to float off the floor to the kitchen, riding on the smell of it.

Tweed got to the kitchen and found Connie in a denim shirt and jeans. There were an unusual number of people there. He said, "Good morning!"

Connie said, "Obviously, you are farther down the hall and weren't wakened by this maddening aroma." She added more honey to the crusty roll in her hand and licked around her mouth like a cream-fed cat.

"How nasty of you not to come and waken me. But no, you had to come down and stuff yourself. You're not only argumentative, you're selfish."

She bit into the gooey mess and said around the mouthful, "Yes."

He got to watch her pink tongue slip out and lick the crumbs and honey stuck on the side of her mouth.

It was disgusting that he had to share that intimacy with the other yahoos around the kitchen. Their faces were soft and indulgent. They'd spoil that woman rotten.

Then he looked at Connie. She wasn't showing off. She didn't even realize that the men were charmed by her. She was unaware that she was the focus of their

attention. She loved the fresh hard roll that was hot
and steaming with melted butter and honey. She was
hungry.

And suddenly Tweed realized that she was comfortable with *men*. It touched in him, and his eyes
prickled. She was going to make it.

She said to Tweed, "Do you realize that I've con-
sented to staying today *and* tomorrow? That I shall
gain ten pounds by the time you take me back to the
hospital for the check up? Will the plane make it with
my added weight?"

His emotional compassion for her recovery made
his voice a little gruff. "I'll let you walk."

She laughed, but all the others said versions of "I'll
take you."

"No," she said airily, "I'll walk. The fifty miles
would probably counter Jake's superb cooking."

Jake chortled.

She continued. "I'd probably meet Gregory along
the way."

And Tweed laughed.

"Who's this—Gregory?" Dusty wanted to know
that.

"Her cousin." That was Tweed's full reply. And he
didn't take his gaze from Connie. To do so would in-
terrupt his appreciation of a work of art.

She was.

He said, "You haven't had the picture tour."

Jake scolded, "She just got up! Give her a little
time." He was busy dishing up potatoes, ham, eggs
and steamed apples. Then, of course, there were the
great pots of coffee. And those rolls. Plus the racks of
newly baked bread. And those pots of honey, rasp-
berry jam and the inevitable grape jelly.

Heaven probably smelled exactly like that kitchen.

Freddy said, "Horse said some yahoo came here looking for Connie. The guy said he was her cousin. It might of been that Gregory you just mentioned."

"Greg?" Connie turned a courteous glance to Freddy.

"Yeah. He called Horse 'boy' and ticked him off. He's short for seventeen."

Still courteous, Connie inquired, "What did he do with Greg?" But she then took another bite from that overloaded roll and closed her eyes with savoring. Everybody watching forgot about Gregory.

# Seven

After breakfast, Connie did insist on just glancing at the computer. Sam uncovered it on its table.

It was like new. Connie commented, "I haven't seen one like that since I was a freshman. It's cumbersome, but it's an excellent basic computer. There's even a template! See? It tells you the basics. And, fellas, it's a snap to run, or program or use. They do have an updated program that's somewhat more sophisticated. While this one is adequate, the newer one would be quicker."

Sam was unconvinced. Tweed showed interest because Connie was interested in the thing. "Sam should be the one who's taught first. If he can do it, then I'll be more confident." He sent Sam a sly look.

"He's just saying that to keep me out from underfoot."

"Right." Tweed's glance, then, was for Connie.

She itched to get at the computer. She begged, "Just let me show you how to use the tutorial for basics. It'll take about twenty minutes. On my honor. You'll know exactly what to do for the completed letter, margins, changes, printing, everything. The printer is connected. You can write letters and print the first out in twenty minutes, or I'll fix supper."

Tweed exclaimed, "That's a nasty goad!"

She ignored Tweed as she became cautious. She asked Sam, "Uhh, can you type?"

Sam laughed. "Reasonably."

She fell back against the library table and put a hand to her chest. "I about had a heart attack. Can you imagine Jake if I went into his kitchen and said I was taking over?"

Sam agreed, "We just had a narrow escape."

So she sat Sam down at the computer and showed him how to turn it on. The computer did that perfectly. The little pulser was eager. Sam was hesitant. She made all sorts of simple mistakes and corrected them. Then she had him do the same mistakes and showed him on the template what to do. Gradually, very gradually, he realized how wonderfully simple it was.

While they both told Sam good luck and goodbye, he gave no indication that they'd ever been there. Like all good hackers, he was already caught.

So the two left the room.

Since it was early, Tweed suggested, "We could go back to bed for a while. You didn't have much sleep last night."

"No, no, no. You promised me a picture tour."

He sighed and put his hands in his pockets. Then he moved his shoulders and indicated the walls with his chin. "Ethel was an artist. A good one. But she attracted and entertained other artists and she bought their pictures. You should see the attic. We gradually weeded out the ones we just couldn't stand any longer, and the ones you see are either Ethel's or ones we like."

"There's a difference?"

"Well, you'll see."

Most of the pictures were the routine ranch, cowboy, barbed wire, cedar post, horse, rope, beef, water barrel, dust-type painting. It didn't take long to sort out Ethel's.

It was Ethel's that Connie studied. She'd had a rowdy humor. She caught men with their pants down, a cow pad on the side of a beautiful and blooming bluebonnet plant, dirty laundry on the line, a tilting outhouse and a guy coming out fixing his shirt into his pants with a clothespin on his nose. There was one of a hard, macho man with a sour, lined face wearing an abused old black Stetson with the Texas state flower, the bluebonnet, in his faded shirt's buttonhole. Those sorts of pictures.

Connie studied Ethel's paintings in silence. Tweed shifted and glanced at her. Connie said, "I wish I'd known her."

Tweed put back his head and laughed.

Connie guessed, "She was outrageous. She must have had Sam on his ear most of the time. She'd be hell to argue with, her humor would get in the way."

Tweed said, "Apparently, from what Sam's said, you've got her exactly right."

And from the door, Sam said, "Yeah." He'd had to hear what Connie would say about Ethel's paintings.

"While I can see her point—the good with the bad, Beauty and the Beast, whatever—in the beauty of the land being—uh—altered by the cow droppings, I must say that I doubt I'd want the cow-chipped bluebonnet hanging on my wall."

Sam said, "You're close, but she meant to show that beauty takes pretty basic applications."

Connie said, "Ahhhh," in closer understanding. She turned to study Sam. "You were both lucky to know each other. She as she was, for you, and you understanding her, for her. How often you must wish you could share things with her."

"Yeah."

Tweed told her, "I love you."

She looked at him and blinked. She didn't scoff or sass, she just smiled in a soft way.

Sam said, "Make him behave."

Neither replied, and Sam went off.

Tweed said, "Kiss me good morning. I can't start the day until you do."

"How have you managed up until now?"

"I never really did."

"If I kissed you, I might forget to eat."

He was very serious. "You've eaten. I made sure."

"Well, then, I suppose I could."

He gave her no more time to debate that. He took her very carefully into his arms; then he devastated her. His arms were hard around her soft body, and his body against hers was an uneven wall of stone. His mouth was greedy and devouring.

Only the fact that he was partially civilized made him lift his mouth and look at her. Her eyes were closed, her face was pale, her body was malleable, limp, boneless. Alarm came into his body in a shock. "Connie...?"

The smile came like the dawn, lighting her face. Her cat's eyes slitted open and she gazed at him with such a smug look.

It could be all right. She wasn't afraid of him. She might even ... come to want him. But he immediately canceled that. For a woman to have endured what she had, to be confronted by another man would be too much. It might be weeks or months or a very long time before she could even consider him. He could wait.

He released her very gently, embarrassed by his greed. He stood her on her feet and said, "You'll need Ethel's boots."

She asked, "Why?"

"I'm going to take you down in the canyon so you can see how it was for primitive people traveling silently and secretly. How far do you think you can walk?"

"In the boots?"

He nodded.

"Oh, two miles?"

"We won't be that long. But I needed to know that you could walk a ways. I'd hate to have to carry you over my shoulder."

"You have weak legs?"

"I gotta have one hand free, so I'd have to carry you over my shoulder, and your stomach could object."

"Why would you have to carry me?"

"If you get to lollygagging along or quit walking, and I'd have to get you back to the car." He seemed perfectly reasonable.

"Why ... one hand free?"

"In case I'd have to...shoot a snake." He'd qual-
ified his reply.

"Is it...always...dangerous out here?"

"Not if you're ready and paying attention."

"Yes." She was quiet as they went up the stairs to
get jackets and ready themselves for the day.

When they met in the upper hall, Tweed was again
wearing a gun belt. He thought of Gregory's being
prepared, and his scornful criticism. Tweed considered that. Well, so was he prepared for unexpected
problems. In a way, it was only the problems that were
varied. While Gregory had pen and paper, Tweed had
a gun. With Gregory it was convenience. With Tweed
it was survival.

Connie again noted the presence of the gun. He
wore it as he wore his hat. It was a part of his clothing. Without it, he would feel undressed.

As they came down the stairs, Jake met them with
a basket. "Morning coffee. She didn't have much for
breakfast."

Tweed took the basket as Connie said, "Thank you,
Jake." And Tweed carried the basket as they went out
to the Jaguar. Tweed put the basket behind the seat
before he helped her inside; then he whistled for Finnigan, who came into the car. There was a rifle on the
rack on the floor of the back seat.

"All the guns. I wished we'd had some."

"Yeah."

"Do you always carry guns?"

"Yeah. This is a big place. We have wild pigs that
are very aggressive. You don't want a wild boar to
catch you walking on the ground. At least you can
choose not to be caught, and if you are caught, you
want to have a reliable gun handy. And on occasion,

you find an injured animal that needs to be released. Then, too, we sometimes have other jackals around."

"Men?"

"Yeah."

"Like those who jumped us."

"Yeah. God, Connie, I wish I'd gotten there sooner."

"Umm." She made a noncommittal sound, but she shook her head slightly.

"Why not?"

"You might have been killed the way my uncle was beaten to death."

"And you, very nearly."

"No."

He wasn't sure if he should go on with that line of talking, so he waited. She looked out of her window and was silent.

But she had referred to the subject of the assaults. Sanford had said the time would come when she would talk about it. It could be anytime, or it might be years. Talking about it was part of the healing process.

Sanford had told Tweed if she should begin to talk, that he should listen. But he hadn't told Tweed how to encourage her to talk or what in God's name he should reply. How could Tweed know what sort of words she might need? His compassion was such that he was tongue-tied.

Tweed wanted only to hold her, to smooth her hair back and kiss her and to make love to her. Men really don't know of any other way to comfort a woman.

The man believes that making love to the woman shows her that he loves her, cares about her and is there. To him, that says everything. Making love to her is a bond. The act satisfies the man and he goes to sleep, while she is left awake with her worries or hovering terrors all still intact.

Tweed knew that God had made men and women to annoy and baffle and fascinate and thrill each other, but understanding either gender by the other is not in their capacity. Tweed had tried. He knew. Why couldn't women be as easy to understand and deal with as another man?

So Tweed and Connie were silent as he drove along the two-track roads to the canyon. He'd gone to another part of it. It was farther from the house. It was more isolated.

He'd questioned Sanford about the isolation. Sanford had replied with some impatience, "Watch her. If she's agitated or restless or nervous, take her back to the car and go back to the house."

So Tweed observed Connie in careful glances.

She didn't appear tense. Her hair blew back under Ethel's Stetson. Her eyelashes were very noticeable. Her head was turned to the window, and he could see the sweet curve of her cheek and how the wind pressed the cloth to her breasts as she looked out at the countryside sliding away past them. What was she thinking?

He didn't know what to say, so he was silent.

They came to an open area of sparse, rocky grassland. There were hills in the distance. There were some cedar trees. The draws that creased the land were lined with cottonwood and an occasional oak. It was high land. Tableland. There were beeves in the distance. Not very many. No human was around that they could see.

They stopped, and Tweed undid his seat belt as he asked Connie, "Do you know where the canyon is?"

She really searched. Putting her hands to her face and stretching, she looked in all directions.

"They're a surprise, all right." He pointed. "It's just ahead there. See that clump of cedars? Then on beyond, you can see some cottonwood bushes. They only look like bushes, those are the tops of trees. They're big trees with their feet down in the water. They have some rock around them, upstream, so they don't get the full force of the gully washers."

"Have you ever been in a gully washer?" She turned her face to him. He saw then that her lashes were wet. She had shed some discreet tears, and his heart was wrung. He opened the door and let Finnigan out to roam. Then he reached over and undid her belt and pushed his seat all the way back. He pulled her over onto his lap, turning her so that her back was to his door. He asked, "What's the matter?"

She hadn't fought him. She hadn't objected.

He leaned over her and his thumb wiped the wet lashes. "Tell me. I can just about fix anything."

She drew a deep, broken breath and laid her head on his left shoulder.

He hugged her to him firmly and said to her, "Ever since I found you, you've never been really alone. Would you like to get out of the car and walk over by that tree and yell at God? There's some times in our lives when that can be necessary. We need to yell up at God and ask him just what the hell was going on and why did that happen and how did He dare to do something like that to us? God does understand those times."

"How do you know?"

"Salty told me."

"Who is he?"

So sitting there in his car in the middle of nowhere, he told Connie about the Brown family, how he got there, what they did, what all *he* did and how they had coped with him. He told her about the inadequate cage and the lecture, and he told about the coat.

She listened.

He told about the kids who had lived with the Browns, and he told about his crush on Carol and he spilled his very guts. He even told about how, just the night before, he'd remembered to thank his mother for having him.

"Salty was lucky to have known you."

He laughed and hugged her. "I was a stiff-spined, nasty-mouthed kid, and it's a wonder Salty ever put up with me."

"What about Felicia?"

"She told me I was a well-made male, that I was handsome and clever. Kinda good cop/bad cop deal between them. They're smart people. When they come down, you'll see what I mean."

"They're going to visit?"

"They have to meet you."

Her eyes saddened. "What if . . . they don't approve of me?"

He took his hand from her hip and gestured openly. "They'll have to hightail it back to Ohio."

Her eyelids covering her sad eyes, she suggested, "Maybe you're prejudiced."

"I've already told you that I love you. Prejudice goes with that. But I've known all along you were perfect. I've never in all my days seen a woman handle herself as you did when I found you. You were awesome. I was envious of you for being so brave."

"I was a basket case."

He shook his head slowly as he told her, "Not until you knew you were safe. I'll bet you would be a tiger with your kids. I'll bet you'd be president of the PTA and chairman of the soup kitchen, and you'd treat your kids and your husband as if you were a pussycat. But you'd be fooling them. You're a woman in control."

She sighed and nodded grimly. "I belong to the Junior League back in Virginia, and they work our tails off."

"Why... I'd *noticed* you didn't have one. So that's what happened to it!"

She shook her head in a disgruntled manner. "Do you realize all you've made me say? Can you understand that you've never had the courtesy to leave me in my cocoon? From the time I first opened my eyes in the hospital, you've shocked me with the things you would say to a woman who was traumatized. You talk and pick at me in such kind ways, and I talk to you."

"And all of your talk has been coherent. No hysteria, no shrieking. You're remarkable."

She ignored his interruption. "Here, I've told you more and listened to more from you than all the hounding people who have so patiently prodded and coaxed. They tried so hard to help me, but they made me shiver and clam up just to think on it all."

"No one else has my patience," he admitted.

"That could be. You wait and listen and talk while you let me slip out little bits and pieces. Pretty soon it will all be emptied out of me, like Snow White's bite of the poisoned apple, and I'll be whole again. Almost." She added that last word sorrowfully.

"What're you missing?"

"I was innocent."

"You were a virgin." He clarified that.

"Yes." Her eyes welled tears. "I'd been honest and behaved myself through all the temptations. And just see what happened. I no longer have the gift of myself that first time to give to the man I love."

"You already gave yourself?"

"I was assaulted."

"So." Gently, he watched her hostile eyes.

She clenched her teeth and stiffened. "I'm not a virgin." Her voice was harsh.

"Is being assaulted your idea of 'giving' yourself? Connie, you didn't give yourself to anyone, as yet. For all practical purposes, you're still an innocent."

"You have strange values."

"Well, it's just possible that you might be overreacting to something that you could not possibly control. If it snowed right now, the car wouldn't start, and I'd have to walk back to the house and maybe fall into the canyon on a rock. Would that be my fault?"

Her eyes were tender. "You should always stay with the car."

"How like a woman to pick at details! Let's see." He squinted at the horizon and saw the beginnings of thunderclouds. "Where'd those come from?"

She jerked up, hitting her elbow on the steering wheel. "What?"

"A storm."

But she looked around anxiously. "Is someone coming?"

"Hey, no one else is anywhere around."

"Where's the dog?"

"A little storm isn't going to bother that dog. It's okay. Settle down. I'm here and I can take care of you."

Her eyes widened and were wild. "Uncle Clyde said that very thing!"

"I'm half as old as your uncle Clyde, and I know this territory. You're safe with me."

*"Uncle Clyde said that, too!"*

Tweed demurred, "He didn't know this territory."

"He hunted here several times every year. How do you think we knew to carry that tire and the flammable oil?"

Soberly, Tweed replied, "I thought the others had lit it."

*"No!* We did! And it brought them to us. We were like trapped birds."

She was sitting up by then, her back to him, her arms wrapped around herself, and she shivered in little tremors. Had he taken her too far?

His mind went frantically for anything to divert her attention. "That storm roiling up. Those are your emotions. You need to shriek and—"

"I did! *I did*—the whole time. No one came." And she collapsed away from him, over her knees, into ragged sobs.

Tweed felt as if he'd foolishly stepped onto a toboggan run, slipped and was hurtling down the icy run with no direction or control. He reached into the back of the car and got a blanket. He wrapped it around Connie and pulled her closely to him as he said soothing words and sounds. He held her through the whole storm, both in and outside the car.

That outside storm was not on any weather map or broadcast he'd heard or read in the last several days.

The lightning flashes and thunder crashes were very appropriate. So appropriate that Tweed wondered if

God was helping Connie to vent all the fury she'd bottled up inside her.

And his compassion shook him, watering his eyes and working his throat, as he held her shuddering body close.

When the sky's storm became less severe and the main turmoil went on its noisy way, so did Connie's personal chaos lessen. She was still upset, but it was more controlled. It was a healing grief. Finally. For her uncle. For their terrible travail.

As both storms began to fade, Tweed found himself rocking her gently, singing odd words to an old nursery rhyme. When had he learned that?

In as soft a voice as he could make his baritone, he half sang, "Hush little baby, don't you sob, Tweed Brown will find you a brand-new job. If that job's a really nasty thing, Tweed Brown will buy you a brand new ring. If that ring has a lousy shine, Tweed Brown will—"

A little voice against his wet neck and shirt collar said a husky, "Those aren't the words at all."

His own voice was husky with his compassion. "Well, now, I can't agree with you there. That's what I was singing and that's my song for you. It's, of course, brilliant. It rhymes. What's the complaint?"

"It begins, 'Hush little baby don't say a word—' And Momma buys her a mockingbird."

"That's what *you* say. But what do women know about nursery rhymes?"

She shook her head and her laugh was a choking gulp. "Oh, Tweed."

"If you're helpless, now's the time to ask you to kiss me. I've been very upset."

"You have!" She was incredulous.

"You've cried all over me, and I was scared of that storm, and you didn't give me any support or hold my hand or anything."

"Sorry."

Soberly, gravely, his voice shaking, he told her, "My love. You turn me inside out. I don't know how to handle my great emotional response to your grief. I never knew your uncle or the kind of man he was. I don't know how to share your grief at all. I hurt for your hurt and I don't know how to communicate that to you. I love you."

"How could you?"

"I fell in love with a woman who was feisty and stood there like a Joan of Arc ready to take on whatever came. She was forced to put on clothes that hadn't belonged to her and she had a rifle pointed right at my heart, *and I knew she wouldn't, couldn't pull the trigger!*"

"See? You've done it again. The clothes. The loathing I felt to have to be covered by their clothes!"

"I know."

"How could you know that?"

"I didn't the first minute, but when I saw how badly you'd been beaten, I knew you weren't wearing what you generally wore. They found none of your things. What happened to them?"

"The others took them. Tweed. Please. My brain won't take any more. I can't think about it any more. Not now."

"Have I told you that you are a brave woman? If I was ever in trouble, I'd want you backing me."

"Don't do this to me."

"Then kiss me."

She made a whimpering sound and lifted her mouth to his, her hand going to the back of his head, and the kiss was cosmic. All that emotion funneled into the kiss, and it got out of control entirely.

They panted and strained and their hands moved and they groaned and shivered and clutched at each other. He warned her, "I'm going to ask for you." He waited and when there was no protest, his husky voice asked, "Will you let me love you?"

And she said, "Oh, Tweed, please."

He hadn't expected that reply. He did hesitate before he carefully rearranged them. Then he remembered to get a condom out of the glove compartment and his hands shook so that he almost couldn't get it on.

He still had enough sense to then kiss her and love her enough so that she was frantic. He even was careful when he put the back of the passenger seat down and laid her on it. Then he made love to her. He made careful, exquisite love to her. It was sweet and tender.

They climaxed in a shudder that probably shivered the car's springs, and they lay spent and exhausted. Still coupled.

She whispered, "So that's what it's like."

His soul groaned. He thought how horrific her experience had been. For her to say those words now, it touched in Tweed such a tender anguish that he was almost sundered. But how could he allow her to look back more fully in comparison? He could not even give her compassion. Not right then. How could he distract her from that thought?

His eyes closed, completely lax, he told her. "I've been coiled up like a too-tightly wound spring since I met you. What have you done to me? Did you break my spring?''

''I hope not.''

Nothing had ever touched him as those three words unmanned him then. He leaked tears, and he kissed her with such gentleness. He whispered words to her and cradled her head in his hands. He looked through his blurred eyes into hers and he said, ''I love you, Connie Moody.''

''Oh, Tweed. How could you? What have we done?''

# Eight

Holding Connie close to him, Tweed repeated, "How could I?" as if to consult with the sages. He was squeezed into that impossible space, partially supported by one elbow. His knees were on the car floor, and his lower legs impossibly distributed under the dashboard. But being couth, he studied her question and tried for a lucid reply. He repeated her question, "How could I?"

He came up with, "I thought you might brag on me for waiting so long."

"*Wait*-ing!" She was baffled.

"Well, I wanted to comfort you in the plane on the way to the hospital, but I didn't know if you could pilot the plane while I was so distracted. I wanted to coax you awake in the hospital. I've wanted you since I first saw you. You ought to gasp at my restraint."

"Restraint!" She was healthily indignant, lying there under him in that cramped space. She said, "Get off me."

He sighed, and still coupled, he lifted his head to look out of the car windows in a leisurely manner. "Boy, you sure lose interest fast. Aren't you the woman who was clawing at me, trying to get at my body? Aren't you the woman who just stuffed me in her?" In an aside, he suggested, "You might cut your nails before the next time."

She was silent.

He looked down into her face and saw that her eyes were misted and her mouth worked. He sobered, "Oh, honey—"

And she ducked her head aside and bit her lower lip. Her tummy shivered and she burst out laughing!

His own eyes watered as he laughed with her. He groaned as he separated from her and complained, "How did you get me into this position? We'll probably have to cut off my legs and reattach them." Then he remembered a conversation with Sanford and he told Connie, "Do you know that Sanford threatened to set my legs at an angle if I didn't quit talking to Betty Lou?"

"What were you saying to her?"

"Hello, goodbye, that sort of thing. Nothing earthshaking like I talk to you. Like saying that I love you."

"Do you realize we made love?"

"I suspected."

"I didn't think I would ever be able to—"

He waited to see if she could go on and say it, but she had stopped. He was opening the door so that he could undo one leg. "You underestimate me."

"What are you doing?"

"I'm trying to solve how I got into this position. How'd we do that? I was over on the other side. There's the console, the brake...well, we did spill the coffee cups."

She again laughed.

He looked at her and smiled. "You got the best laugh. I haven't heard it that way. You've smiled and chuckled a time or two, but that's a great laugh."

"You are an impossible man."

"And you're no help at all. How the hell am I to get off you? I know." He moved his upper body enough to release her; then he turned his shoulders, put his head out the door and put his hands on the door sill so that he could crawl out of the car. He sat on the ground in some disarray and looked at her. "That just isn't a couth way to leave a lover. We probably ought to try a bed."

"Or the ground?" She was sitting up on the reclining seat and watching him.

He tested the spring of the solid rocky ground and observed, "A bed has more bounce."

"You like...bouncing?"

"It's like golf. You need to follow through."

And she had to lie back to laugh.

The whole episode was very emotional for Tweed. He'd had no idea of actually making love with Connie. His only goal had been to get her out into the dreaded countryside, to accept being away from people and out of the car. To feel the freedom of space. Not to be afraid.

He was a little, just a tad, naw, he wasn't at all sorry they'd made love. He looked at her laughing and he smiled. She was a strong woman. She would finally be all right. Maybe not tomorrow. Maybe not in a month, but eventually she would be all right again.

She'd apparently had no nightmares the night before. That morning, the sleeping pill had still been on her bedside table.

He got up stiffly and removed the condom. He bent to bury it and saw that the ground was dry! With all that fury, the storm had gone on without leaving any needed water on the ground.

That spooked Tweed a little, and he looked at the sky. It was serene. Had the storm been his imagination? Had his empathy to Connie conjured the storm?

He looked around as men always did wherever they were, and the whole place was placid. He saw Finnigan about two city blocks away, watching him, waiting to see if he was needed. When Tweed didn't whistle, the dog disappeared again.

Tweed dropped the used condom down a crack in the ground and scooped some dirt down over it. He zipped up his jeans before he contemplated the lazy woman lying back on the reclined seat and watching him.

He said, "I hate to spoil you this way, but we have a brunch waiting for us? We have to taste everything," he explained. "So while I know you want to tussle again, we will have to have at least a bite of each thing so that we can tell Jake what it was like. Understand? It's not that I wouldn't want to accommodate you again, you realize, it's just that we have to pamper Jake and make him feel needed, so he doesn't sulk."

"What's he do when he sulks? Who cooks?"

"Oh, *he* does, but he boils cabbage, potatoes and corned beef all together and—"

"I like that."

"Well, we do, too, but not every meal."

She sighed in resignation. "I suppose we might as well get at it."

"Again? You're voracious!"

"The food."

Tenderly, he told her, "You're food for the gods."

"Oh, Tweed, you are so sweet."

"Naw, take a bite, I'm stringy and sour. You're the sweet one."

"I—" She smiled. "I won't say it. We'd just get into that awful position again, and you might get leg cramps." Then she considered, "Well...I could drive us back, and the boys could extract you next time. They would be so interested in how you got into that position."

"You're just the kind of woman who'd do that and stand around looking innocent and concerned so they couldn't laugh until they got away. They'd just snort and cough and have a terrible time."

Primly, she announced, "It's good discipline not to be able to do as you choose, when you choose, all the time."

"Laugh?"

"Make love."

"Now that isn't discipline, that's torture. I've just learned that the hard way. Did you get that? The hard—"

"I did hear. You seize on every opportunity to—"

"I try. God knows that I try."

"To make the worst possible salacious references."

"Golly! I didn't know it was that impressive. And speaking of im-press-ive, I have an idea."

"It isn't an idea with you, it's an obsession. Your mind works on turning anything into an innuendo."

He took a quick breath and opened his mouth.

"Don't touch that word."

He leaned his head back and laughed at the sky.

He finally got out the picnic basket, and she spread the cloth. Tweed could not believe the variety of the dainties Jake had concocted. "Jake must have been up all night long to make these things. I am impressed."

"We should give him a gift in return. This is marvelous."

"Okay. We'll have a party and let him control the food."

"No, I meant something *for* him."

"He's peculiar, he likes to show off, the more he can cook for, the happier he is...although he acts like the burdens of the world rest on his doing it all. It's a nuisance having such a cook, but the food is scrumptious. That's how we keep the crew that works here. We don't pay them anything at all, we just let Jake feed them."

"We? I thought Sam owned this outfit."

"I've bought in. I think I own a whole acre by now. I turn my wages back to him each month, and he tells me what part I own. It's in a ruined draw. Nothing grows there but scrub pine. No crop. The taxes must be horrendous on the good land if that's what I pay on mine."

"You're teasing."

"Yeah. Sam and I have been like family since I came here. I've had a room in the house all along. He treats the crew like they're pros. They are. We've got a good bunch."

"Sam has a good partner."

"Sam's a good man. The crew's young. The drought and economy slowdown made the older crew members leave us. There wasn't the work for them to support themselves well enough. Sam settled with them. He puts aside money for each man and he gives it to them when they leave. It was starter money for somewhere else. These men will begin to marry and settle in. We hope the market changes, the rains are kind and we get busy again."

"I'm a good accountant, and I work free. I owe you my life."

"Well, I intend getting returns on that obligation that have nothing to do with you working outside of my bed."

"I have a master's in business. I could help. I could organize your files and make it easier for you. I could set up a chart of accounts, you could keep your financial records on the computer so that you could know the state of your business. You could have a three-year business plan in the computer, and then you could judge how you're doing compared to the projections in the plan."

"Everything you say makes good sense. It's only logical to use the electronic genius of a computer. I'm not geared to it, and no one else has shown any interest in that wasted machine. My share in the business isn't pivotal. I'll back you, but Sam is the boss. Let's talk to Sam."

"You would take to a computer like one of your ducks to water."

"Good. We'll go swim in the lake and ask the ducks about computers." Then he asked, "Have you been paying attention to what you're eating? Remember.

You got to tell Jake something about *every*thing in that basket."

"I know. I know! Don't distract me."

"Jake makes eating a chore. He looks so intense until you say something. We delay at times just to make him sweat."

"The whole bunch of you is just terrible."

"Yeah." Tweed laughed.

"You need movies for the VCR."

"You can't see the movies they got for the VCR."

"I won't ask why."

"No, it isn't that so much as we don't get into town very often and we've memorized the dialogue."

"Nonsense."

"Okay. You'll find out. You join the outfit, you have no choice but the video library we've collected. You'll be just as bad as all the rest. The worst part is where there isn't any dialogue and the guys tell what's going to happen. They don't have to do that. We all *know* what's going to happen, but some jackass will do it anyway."

"What a terrible time you've had, having to watch old films."

"It gets really wild."

"Wild?"

"Once Jake threw a glass of beer at Rusty, and it ended up in a water fight. It was a riot! We ignored the film, running along and useless. And we took sides and matched up. We were really a mess. Sam wouldn't let us back inside, and it was winter."

"A TEXAS winter? That's no punishment."

"Honey, you obviously never experienced a TEXAS blue norther. They're wicked. The wickedest weather ever visited on poor, defenseless people."

She sassed, "The temperature must drop...oh... clear down to forty degrees?"

He was serious. "It's sudden and bitterly cold. It drives the cattle ahead of it. They freeze piled against any barrier, a fence or rocks. And the snow piles up over them. We don't find them until it thaws. Talk about stink."

"That must be a tough time."

"Not for vultures, carrion eaters and wolves."

"I suppose any life has a balance of good and bad."

He stopped eating and just looked at her.

Their exchange of regard wasn't lost on her. She finally said, "Yes. Even for me."

"You know that and you've got a leg up on every other problem you'll ever face."

"Uncle Clyde..."

"Sanford said Clyde had inoperable cancer."

"Ahh. So that was why he suggested this trip and it had to be now."

"Things balance."

"What would you say if he hadn't been so ill?"

"That things still balance. There would be a reason. I hate to think you lost your uncle just so's I could know you. Find you. Love you."

"Oh, Tweed."

"Or it could have been so's I'd leave Betty Lou alone so that Sanford looked good to her."

"So, Betty Lou caught your eye?"

"I never had a chance. He saw her every single day and flirted and complimented and scolded and bossed her. How's a guy to compete with something like that?"

"Did you love her?"

He considered her question. "I probably could have. I did hanker after her a little, but then I met you, and Betty Lou was just a nice girl."

"Hadn't she been 'nice' before that?"

Tweed laughed out loud. Then he said, "Are you getting jealous? Good! But there's no need. Betty Lou will be a good friend to you all the rest of our lives."

"She'll come see me in Virginia?"

"She'll come out to the ranch, and you'll go see her wherever they live."

"They?"

"She and Sanford."

"So you've paired them off?"

"He did. And he was really hard-nosed about it. He couldn't even see any humor in my talking to her."

"What about my talking to him?"

He smiled at Connie. "When I was trying to get you to wake up, I almost got into bed with you and kept you there."

"You were never in the room alone with me until after I wakened."

"A minor detail."

She considered Tweed. "You're an arrogant man."

"No. Not at all. There are other men who know more and can do more and can make things happen. I'm only me. But I don't mind telling you that I approve of myself and my motives. I like myself, but then, I'm not intolerant of other men. So maybe I'm no judge of myself. I think the fact that I breathe and live in this world, and know you, are all miracles. Salty is another, but he can't match you."

"I hope I'm here when Salty and Felicia come down."

Tweed bit into something odd looking from the tray and considered it as he replied with soft calm, "You'll be here."

"Let's get back to the house and see how Sam is doing with the computer." She looked at her watch. "He's been at it for over two hours."

"I have to kiss you a couple of times before I can drive the car. I wouldn't mind kissing you and driving, but you might possibly complain about having to sit on the console or on my lap."

"Quite possibly. Can you drive and kiss a woman like that?"

"We could see."

She laughed at him. And her laugh was to his ears what ambrosia was to the tongue.

So he dragged her willing body over to him and spent some time showing her the ways that a man could kiss a woman. She was limp, red lipped and sleepy eyed and a little mussed up when he sat back hot eyed and restless.

They put the remnants from the brunch out for the birds and animals. As they shook out the cloth and refolded it, Tweed said, "I wonder if Jake is a runaway who's wanted somewhere. Why would a man who can cook and bake like he does be out here at the far end of forever, wasting his culinary talents on the desert air?"

She noted the reference. "You read."

He shrugged. "And write! I can count to a hundred, too, but I can't operate that computer."

"You can kiss, and touch, and love a woman senseless."

"Hey! Do you think that could be marketable?"

"No."

And he laughed.

They called Finnigan, who returned with some interest. They put him into the back seat, got inside the car themselves and each gave a remembering look at the area. He took her hand and said to her seriously, "It was here that we first made love. I think I'll put up a monument."

"Oh, Tweed." Then she asked rather carefully, "What sort of monument?"

He looked around as he drove and suggested, "Like something on a bachelor's party cake?"

"Oh, my word."

He was sure. "Honey, we're not talking words here, we're talking about your wiggly, sly and alluring body, your wicked kisses and your curious hands."

"My hands mind their own business."

"Hah! I'll probably have to wear a sling for weeks!"

She covered her flaming face with her hands, but she bubbled laughter.

And he would glance over at her, smug and pleased as he drove along the track.

They got back to the house and no one was anywhere around. Tweed put the picnic basket in the kitchen. Jake was gone. That was strange. Jake was always in the kitchen at that time of the day.

Tweed took Connie through the house, calling to Sam, and there was no reply. Tweed frowned.

They went into the office and found the computer covered. There were about ten letters in the mail basket that had all been printed from the computer!

Connie exclaimed, "He did it!"

"You'll have to teach him how to address the envelopes." Tweed picked up the letters and glanced at them. "No errors. I am impressed."

She asked, "Where is everyone?"

"I'll look at the board." Tweed went outside and checked the board. It was roofed and there was a blackboard where messages were left. It said, "Fire in the far west acreage below the canyon. Pete's at the hangar. Jake's in town. We can handle it."

Tweed said, "We have the house to ourselves."

"Is there a fire?"

"Yes. Sam never finagles."

"Finagles?"

"Is that a strange word to you? It means to fool."

"Good word."

"Come back inside. I'll show you a thing or two."

"You already have."

"I'll show you the tweed coat."

"That would be worth the risk."

"What—risk?"

"Going into an empty house with you after you've eaten. You could do anything."

"Like what?" he asked, politely curious.

"Like sleep the rest of the afternoon?"

He grinned at her.

"What did you think I'd say?" She smiled just a trifle and watched him.

"I thought you'd lure me to your room."

"The bed's made up."

He said, "We could remake it."

"Are you propositioning me?"

"Why...do you suppose I'd do something crass like that?"

"Yeah," she replied.

"You're right. Let's hurry while we have the chance."

So it was late that afternoon before Tweed, indeed, showed Connie the ordinary, worn, precious tweed coat.

The others came back to the house. They were all tired and tarnished with black soot, sweat and dirt. The two who had been holding the house against intruders were fixing steaks and baked potatoes and a humongous salad. There were still Jake's rolls from that morning.

The men washed at the outside faucet and came inside without changing from the clothing they'd worn. They were weary warriors. And they were starved.

They greeted the pair with envious eyes, and they sat silently and ate every crumb put before them. Then they went to the showers and to bed. They'd had a rough day.

Before Sam ate, he had insisted stubbornly to Tweed that it would be he who took back the hot food to the two men left at the fire site. He took that, iced tea, water and bedrolls.

Jake finally came back from town. On a curve, avoiding an armadillo, he'd slid into a rock and broken a wheel. He'd had to be towed into town. "It was interesting. I rode in the cab with Terry Spendlier. Remember him? Do you know his sister went to Fredricksburg and married her cousin? Her cousin! She was strange enough, but to compound it by marrying a cousin? What sort of children will they have?"

The two lovers helped Jake to unload and store the foods purchased. Then Jake looked at the chaos in his kitchen. "Who cooked?" Not "what happened" or "who was the cook," but just who had cooked?

Connie promised hastily, "We just aren't as familiar with the kitchen as you. We will clean it up."

Jake pleaded earnestly, "Promise you won't do that, it's enough of a mess as it is."

Sam came in then, and he, too, was very tired. He said to Connie, "That machine is magic. I could kick myself for not having even looked at it before now. Thanks."

He ate the meal that Jake quickly prepared for the tired man. Then Sam, too, had showered and gone to bed.

It had been a hard day for everyone but the lovers. They exchanged a glance and went back to bed together.

They whispered and smothered giggles and breathed carefully, openmouthed, to silence themselves.

They luxuriated in having the freedom of exploring each other and of tasting one another. It was a bacchanalia without the wine.

He claimed his kisses were two-way range finders. She couldn't understand what he was talking about. He explained that his kisses were a monitor to judge her recovery.

"What—recovery?"

He vacillated, "From sexual encounters." That wasn't lying, but it wasn't avoiding what he was saying, either.

And her kisses loosened. She wasn't quite so cautious. She didn't stiffen and force herself to relax. She was easier with him. He was sweet and loving with her.

Breathily, she asked, "Who taught you to kiss that way?"

"What way?" he questioned.

"You make my knees buckle."

"Let me see." And he went down under the sheet to test her knees, and one thing led to another.

But he had to come up along her body to kiss her so that her gasps could be muffled. He told her, "You shouldn't shriek like that."

And she cooled.

It was only then that he remembered she'd said she'd shrieked all the while that she was being assaulted . . . and no one had come to help her.

He held her and petted back her hair, and he didn't do anything else. She was silent. He simply held her. He didn't ask her anything because she hadn't said anything. He didn't dare to ask her if she was mad at him or if she wanted to go back to her own bed. She might go. He just held her and was silent.

And when she finally began to relax and even later when she slowly slid into sleep, he continued to hold her, his eyes looking at the night, his face very serious.

Tweed knew the time would come when she wouldn't remember so clearly, and that time could be years away. But that day had been an amazing step in her recovery. She would again be whole. That time would come.

It would be a while.

In the meantime, she would be with him.

For the rest of their lives, they'd be one entity. He would care for her and about her. He would love her. He already did.

How could he know that?

He was the first man who had come to her help in that hollow. Maybe she was only grateful to him.

Maybe she didn't actually care about him. What if she was only clinging to him because he had come to her and he was protective of her.

He lay in the dark with that dear woman in his arms and against his hot body. He wondered if, when she healed, she would be strong enough to leave him.

He considered that soberly as he stared into the night. He knew he couldn't give her up. How could he bind her to him so tightly that she wouldn't think of leaving him?

He understood that he was selfish. Just because he liked that particular place, he recognized that it might not be the choice for a woman. She could be lonely there. And the loneliness could very well remind her of that isolated hollow.

How could he be sure that she didn't cling to him just because she'd been so terrified, and he was somebody to hold on to so that she could feel safe?

Was he only a safety net? Another enclosed, protected space?

And Tweed doubted that he could be enough for such a woman. He had been discarded all his life. From his mother all the way through— No, it had been he who had left the Browns.

But he'd kept their name. And he'd kept Salty's tweed coat.

Then he considered his life and he thought of all he'd accomplished. He was a man who stood on his own feet, and he was an honest, hardworking man who now held a place in the world.

He would convince her to stay. Or he would go wherever she wanted to be.

# Nine

The next morning, Tweed wakened with a dead arm and a cramped body. He turned his head very carefully and saw that Connie still slept.

She was beautiful. With the hospital stay, her tan had faded so that her skin was almost translucent. Her parted lips were soft and slightly pink. Her tan-colored eyelashes were longer than they appeared. Her brows were arches of decoration.

He lifted the sheet very carefully and looked down her naked body. How amazing was a woman's body. Lax and sprawled, she was so alluring that he swallowed rather noisily.

"Just what are you doing?" she whispered.

He turned his head quickly and saw that she was still lax, her eyes were still closed. How long had she been awake, and why had she lain there silently if she'd known he was awake? "I had to lift the sheet to verify the fact that you're on my side of the bed. You're selfish and argumentative, and I don't know how I ever put up with you."

"You like me naked and available," she guessed in almost silent words.

Matching her discretion, he elaborated her words, "You have to realize that I also like you clothed and unavailable. This craving I have for you doesn't come on me just now and then when you deliberately tempt me like you're do—"

Still lax, with her eyes closed, she hissed through almost closed lips, "I was not!"

So in a soft-soft voice he inquired, "Then why didn't you say, 'Good morning,' instead of just lying there, looking like a goddess that could turn a man into a goat man?"

"Why would I want you to be a goat man?"

His breaths hot, he whispered, nuzzling along her shoulder, "Haven't you ever read about nymphs and satyrs? We have words that come from them. Nymph is delicious sex and satyrs are humorous. Do you laugh at me?"

"I'm afraid to move, you might jump me."

"Now why would you think I'd do a thing like that? I have a paralyzed arm—"

She opened her eyes and looked at him. Right into his eyes. His were blue volcanoes of desire and there were yellow fire flashes of humor. What a combination!

Hardly breathing, she inquired, "What's the matter with your arm?"

"You slept on it all night, and I can't feel anything."

"Then why are you moving your hands over me that way, if you can't feel anything?"

"I thought you might restore the fingers' sensitivity."

She breathed. "Hah!"

He chided in quietened words, "You make me sound like a greedy man."

She smothered sounds of her humor.

So he kissed along as he chose, and he cautioned her, "Shh. Everybody is listening."

"What do you mean?"

"All of the men out in the bunkhouse are lying awake, wondering just what you're doing."

"Nonsense."

"It isn't either nonsense. If you weren't here in my bed, I'd be awake and wondering."

"You're peculiar."

"No. No." He slowly shook his head rather elaborately. But his face was against the bottom of her ribs, so his forehead nudged against the bottoms of her breasts.

She added, "And marauding."

He rubbed his face and his morning beard along under her breasts as his hot breath just about scalded her flesh. He replied, "Now why would you think I'm...a marauder? Doesn't that mean a man who captures things?"

"Yes." Connie breathed the word.

"I didn't know that. What do I get for me?"

"Right now, nothing. I'm not interested."

"Good." His satisfied word was almost silent. "Then I can root around and explore you without having to be constantly fending you off."

No woman can giggle closemouthed. Connie could.

While she kept mentioning that she wasn't interested, there were those little gasps and sighs, and she did move in little writhings that drove him crazy. He whispered crossly, "Hold still!" And he whispered, "Don't do that!" And he whispered, "How'd your hand get there?" And he whispered, "Cut that out!" And he whispered, "Why, Constance Moody! Shame on you!"

She didn't say anything at all.

They spent some time trying to silence their breathing, moving stealthily, shivering and sweating. They'd been somewhat distracted and hadn't heard the buzzing of the plane that had landed on their field.

As they lay back—finally—and gradually relaxed and recovered, there were no sounds. Well, they did hear the ducks out by the pond, the birds, a sneaky mockingbird who was pretending to be a canary, and a horse clopping at a distance. Then there was the smooth sound of a motor as a car or truck came steadily closer.

"A car?" She turned her head to watch Tweed with lazy eyes.

"A Ford truck."

"How can you tell it's a Ford?"

"All real TEXANS drive Fords."

Logically, she inquired, "Why?"

"It's in the state constitution."

"Well, for goodness' sakes!"

"Yeah. It's a law. In this great state, only the non-TEXANS drive something else." Then he mentioned, "That's our truck from the hangar. We've got company."

They heard as the truck stopped and the motor was shut off. The truck doors slammed. Both doors. There were two people. Then there were footfalls coming toward the house. The listeners heard the screen door squeak open and slam as Sam went out onto the porch. And they heard men greeting each other.

"That's Sanford," Connie exclaimed very quietly as she began to get up.

"What's he doing here?"

"Has he come to fetch me back?"

"No. There weren't any arrangements for anyone else to do that. I'm supposed to fly you back tomorrow, but I don't see—"

"Who's that with him?" Connie was sitting up, her face serious, listening at a distance.

"Sounds like the sheriff."

"No."

"What's the matter?"

"They've come to see me, and they'll question me."

He countered that idea. "There're other things around that have happened. You're not the only problem around."

She looked at Tweed. "Problem?"

"All sorts of things bring the sheriff out of town. Poachers, fences, disputes, runaways, loose cattle, you'd be astonished what all a sheriff has to do."

"He doesn't take Sanford along on those kinds of things."

"You think they want to question you again?"

She shivered.

"Honey, you don't realize how strong you are. Sanford won't allow the sheriff to hound you, and neither will I. I think we'd better get dressed. I'd be uncomfortable if they came up here and accosted us like we are now. But I would be a little smug to have them find you in my bed."

"Cretin."

"I happen to know what that word means and I am inclined to agree with the label, but I've compromised you to the point that you will have to consider me very seriously."

She gave him a dismissive glance and left his bed. With Sam on the front porch, she was just about positive that she could make it to the bathroom without anyone catching her coming out of Tweed's room.

She did that.

It was such an old house that there were lavatories in the bedrooms, and Tweed rinsed himself off, splashing around, giving himself thoughtful glances in the mirror, frowning. Why were those particular men down there? Why had they come? What had they discovered? What was yet another serious questioning going to do to Connie?

So Tweed was dressed and waiting at the top of the stairs for Connie when she finally came from her room. They exchanged a serious look, their eyes troubled. Both dreaded having to allow the healing in Connie to be tampered with at all. At least for now.

She had made love with Tweed. It still amazed him that she had allowed him that intimacy after whatever she'd endured in the hollow. She was healing. She could now passionately join with him, showing no seeming hesitancy.

She had slept two nights without a sleeping pill. The two wanted earnestly to be past what had happened to her in that hollow. She wanted to forget it.

The authorities wanted to know who had killed the two men. What had happened to their car? Who had taken their clothing and possessions? Where had the rifle come from? What had really happened?

The investigators did know, now, that Clyde Moody and his niece had been stalled in the hollow. It had been Clyde who had set the signal tire on fire the first time. They knew that because she had told the story to Tweed the day before, and he had reported it to the sheriff.

Tweed was a little restless, wondering if the sheriff would have enough tact not to mention to Connie that he already had that information—and from Tweed.

If the sheriff did tell and Connie became aware that Tweed had been passing on information about her, she could slam her defenses down and shun Tweed Brown. The idea of becoming alienated from her scared Tweed.

As the lovers went down the stairs, they could hear Sam saying to the visitors, "Come on in for coffee. Have you eaten? Jake's got a few scraps left."

The sheriff replied, "I'll take Jake's scraps over my wife's banquet anytime. Uh-h-h-h. Don't tell her I said that."

His two listeners smiled politely.

Then Sanford came into the house and saw Connie and Tweed waiting, sober faced and silent.

Seriously, he gave Connie intense looks of evaluation as he said, "Good morning."

Tweed replied as the others came inside and added their greetings to the pair. Tweed nodded to each of the other two and added sober responses. But Connie was silent.

Sanford said, "The sheriff had to come out this way, so I came along, just checking up on you to see if you're all right." He studied the faint whisker burns around Connie's mouth and he relaxed. If she was allowing Tweed to kiss her that seriously, she was doing okay. Well, better.

The sheriff, too, observed those faint, betraying marks. He said, "Come and sit with us. Have you had breakfast?"

Tweed replied, "Not yet."

Under any other circumstances, such a remark from a rancher, at that late-morning ranch hour, would have drawn smiles or chortles or ribald remarks. However, under those circumstances, no one said anything.

They went into the kitchen and on beyond to the screened porch. They all sat at the table. There were cups of hot coffee already waiting for them, put there by Jake, who had noted the arrivals and knew that Sam would invite the men in for a second breakfast.

The four men ate as they exchanged area news in a casual manner. Connie wasn't actually listening—except for the expected questions that she was braced to endure. Her lips were pale and her skin was whitened by her tension. She picked at her food.

Sanford kept his eyes from her enough. But he did look at her, and he was becoming more and more sure that they should leave her alone a little longer. She was better, there was no question about that, but she wasn't ready for the questions the sheriff was impatient to ask.

Even before they had finished their meal, Tweed said, "Duke brought in those beeves we told you about. You'll want to see them. They either were lost from a load somewhere, or they got loose and wandered some distance. Like we told you, they don't have any brands. That's strange, but they don't."

There was no better way to mark a lie than to say that there were unbranded beeves. It was that bald falsehood which Tweed used to tell the two men that he wanted them away from Connie.

After the first little hesitation over such a thing, the two visitors went right on chewing, talking and acting like what Tweed had said was perfectly normal.

Sanford asked Connie, "Do you want to go back with us?"

She looked shocked and her lips parted as she quickly looked at Tweed.

Sanford noted that, and he continued placidly, "If they can tolerate you, you could stay a couple more days. I can see you haven't been harmed by being here." His face was bland and his voice sounded sincere. He did not exchange even a flicker of a glance with Tweed.

Sam said, "She's teaching me the computer. We'll need her here for a month or so."

"Is that acceptable to you, Connie?" The sheriff was frowning.

"Yes." She said that instantly and through very pale lips.

The sheriff questioned, "You feeling okay? You look a little peaked."

"I'm fine."

And suddenly, unexpectedly, the sheriff asked, "There were five men came there, right?" The sheriff had bluntly slid that right in. The silence was tense.

"Yes."

Unexpected questions can sometimes unbottle response. "How many left in your uncle's car?"

"Three." She shivered.

Tweed put his arm around her and glared at the sheriff.

"Can you describe them?"

"They were dressed in work clothes and wore straw, Stetson-like hats."

"Did they call each other by name?"

"No." She shook her head, but she frowned and was distracted.

"Did they take your jewelry?"

"Yes. The opal ring and a watch."

"Anything else? Anything to lead us to them? Were they the ones who beat your uncle?"

"No."

Sanford said, "That's enough."

The sheriff went on, "If you remember anything, no matter how slight it is, you call me. Day or night. Understand?"

"Yes."

"We want those bastards."

"Yes."

"Are you really all right here, or should you go back to the hospital for a while? You could come back, if you want to. We can take you with us now."

"No."

Sanford again said, "That's enough."

"I just want her to know we care about her."

It was Connie who responded. "I know."

"Good."

Sanford looked at his watch. "We need to get back."

"Yeah." The sheriff stretched. "Jake, you get tired of Sam's picky appetite, you come back to town. I'd hire you full-time."

Jake snorted. "You'd look through all the wanted posters and find one that might pass for me, and you'd make me a wageless trustee and allow me to cook for you."

"That about says it all." The sheriff laughed big.

Sanford chuckled nicely, and Sam gave a friendly slap to the sheriff's shoulder.

Tweed said, "Fly low and slow, going back. Be careful."

The two travelers looked at Tweed knowing he didn't want any burning-tire smudges on the horizon to remind Connie of her own ordeal.

"Speaking of getting lost—" the sheriff stretched again and got comfortable "—we found a yahoo wandering around looking for the Comstock Road. We told him he was on it. His name is Gregory Moody. Some kin?" The sheriff lifted inquiring eyebrows at Connie.

"A cousin."

"He said Tweed had given him the directions and, unfortunately, he mentioned you'd been standing there at the time, so we figured neither of you wanted him out here, so we sent him north to the Chisholm Trail. It'll be an enlarging experience for him."

For a change, it was Sam who corrected, "Diminishing experience. He's driving a rental car."

"Now, how do you know that?"

"He came by here and called Horse 'boy,' and that really ticked Horse. Short as he is, he's got proof he's a man. He sent the tenderfoot on a wild-goose chase."

"How un-TEXAN!" The sheriff *tsked* and shook his head. Then he reached for the toothpick holder, selected one and proceded to clear his teeth in a reflective way before he asked Connie, "Do you really want to stay with these buzzards?"

"Yes." She looked at the sheriff steadily.

So he got hearty. "Well, if they get unruly, you can always light a—torch." He'd come that close to mentioning a signal tire. He floundered, proving that he was sensitive to what he'd almost said. Heavily jovial, he blundered on, "They're the type that'd rip the phone off—"

Tweed shifted rather violently in his chair and cleared his throat.

The sheriff appeared to realize he was making it worse and stopped. Then he looked straight at Connie and said very seriously, "They'll take good care of you."

Even more pale, Connie said, "Yes."

The others finished the meal with dispatch and spotty conversation. Nothing was said about questioning Connie any further. Not after that. The sheriff obviously felt terrible. He said his goodbyes, clomped out of the house and just went to the truck.

Sanford asked, "Any nightmares?"

She shook her head.

"Take some time. No one wants to spook you."

Tweed stood by. No taller than Sanford, he appeared to loom in a very hostile way.

Sanford indicated Tweed with a tilt of his head and inquired of Connie, "He giving you any trouble?"

She put her arm through the crook of Tweed's and said, "No."

But Sanford wasn't fooling when he warned Tweed, "Take care of her."

Tweed just looked at Sanford steadily and did not reply.

Tweed walked out to the truck with the two men and Sam. It was then that the sheriff told him, "We heard of two men roaming and prowling in the area south of here. They're not from around here. They're drifters and say so. We have no information on them."

Sam asked, "Driving or on foot?"

"They're driving a rusty blue twelve-year-old Ford pickup. They have a transfer title to the truck. We can't find any place they call home. We find them suspicious."

And again it was Sam who asked, "You think they might be the ones from the hollow?"

"That car, left down there, had cocaine in the panels."

Sam asked, "You left the drugs there?"

"Naw. But there are traces. It could look like their own men took it out and replaced the panels."

"So you're not sure about the two?"

"They may just be drifters. We can't find anything on them. From what we can find, nobody's looking for them. We're keeping track. You never can tell. They wear work clothes just like all the hands around here, and they're wearing straw Stetson-like hats. Help us keep a sharp eye out."

Sam said, "Thanks for the warning. I'll tell the boys. They may be looking for stray cattle they can haul off in a discreet way."

"Like that unbranded bunch Tweed talked about?"

Tweed said sourly, "I was warning you not to push her."

"We know that."

And Tweed said harshly, "Why'd you do that? What did you learn that you hadn't already figured out from the boot marks and the other car tire tracks?"

The sheriff explained, "We now know the three didn't kill the uncle, and she confirmed the jewelry."

Tweed declared, "There were print marks by the cattle across the exit tire marks. Those beeves were through there three days before I found Connie. The bodies weren't dead that long."

The sheriff was firm. "We need confirmation."

Tweed said sourly, "You already had it from the investigation of the site."

"We want to know who killed the other two. Connie? Her uncle? In the condition he was, how could he? Or did someone happen on them and take revenge for her?"

Tweed promised, "If I ever find out that happened, I'll protect his identity with my life."

"A good, law-abiding man." The sheriff was disgusted. "We need to tidy up this mess and get it put away. We still haven't found the Moody car, their clothing, luggage, money, nothing but her empty purse."

"Her uncle's dead, the two attackers are dead, and Connie could heal if she wasn't being badgered. The car and luggage are worthless."

"Three men left a woman and man to die at the hands of two other men. Those two killed the man and were enjoying the woman before they killed her or just left her there. Or. Were those three going to come back and enjoy what was left of her? When criminal acts are executed, we have to find the criminals. We don't want those three showing up and surprising somebody else out here."

Sam asked, "Like those two you're watching?"

"We're giving them a frustrating time."

Sam warned, "We'll take our turn in watching the hollow, but don't let them distract you from something going down somewhere else."

"We've thought of that, too."

Tweed knew the sheriff. He'd known him for some time and he'd always seemed a buffoon. But now, as the man talked and explained, his manner was different. Tweed watched him and wondered if he acted the casual, clumsy part in order to find out what he wanted? With his explanation of the events and his careful relentlessness, he was revealing something of the true man. People are fascinating. Tweed narrowed his eyes and watched the different man.

When the sheriff and Sanford had driven away, Tweed stood beside Sam and watched them leave. Tweed said to Sam, "The sheriff is a fooler."

"Most men are."

"What was his purpose in—almost—referring to the burning tire?"

"He wanted to rattle her."

"He almost made her faint."

"He wanted to know if she was strong enough for some real questions. He needs to know exactly what happened down there in the hollow."

"Oh," Tweed groaned and put his head down to his hands. "My poor, sweet girl."

Sam then had the confirmation that Tweed loved Connie. "So."

"Yeah."

"You need to help. She needs to get this poison out of her so it isn't just healed over and the pus will cause her nightmares and senseless fears for a debilitating time."

"How do you know that could happen?"

"I've asked."

Disgruntled, Tweed said, "I didn't think of anything but making it easy for her to see me."

"And you did that quite well. You sure as hell had better be serious about her."

"Sam, for Pete's sake!"

"Well, you can tell me."

"I have to get her to the point where I can tell her first! You always rush things."

"I want to see it done."

Tweed was exasperated. "I'm working on it!"

"You're too damned slow."

"She's only been out here three days. And this is only the start of the third day."

"It's half-over. If you hadn't lolled around in bed all morning, you'd know that."

"Sam, you're nosey."

"Ethel's ghost had a cattle prod on me to get you two together."

"From what I've heard about Ethel, she's more subtle than that."

"If you expect to do justice to lunch, you two had better go and swim around in the pond. You don't have a whole lot of time to work up a decent appetite, and I won't have you two offending Jake and not eating his food and making him go into one of his snits. I'm too old to handle that much stress." He stomped off. Then he turned and lectured, "Don't dive deep, the water's cold on the bottom."

So... what was Tweed to do? After hunting everywhere else, he found Connie with the computer. He gave her Sam's orders. She frowned at Tweed and didn't take her hands from the keyboard. She said, "Go away."

So Tweed explained how Jake could go into a snit and Sam said he was too old to cope with Jake under those circumstances, so it was up to them to exercise until they could eat a reasonable amount for lunch.

"Don't worry," she replied, "I didn't eat any breakfast, I'll make up for both of us at lunch."

So since she'd referred obliquely to the stress, Tweed felt free to say, "Are you okay?"

"Yes."

"I know a great relaxer."

"That again."

"What?" he asked in all innocence. "What do you think I meant?"

"Back to bed?"

"Well, if you want to tussle around with me, there's the hay stack in the far barn. Let's go try that. You ought to use these times for variety and experimentation because after it's legal, I'll want to do it only in bed."

"Really?"

"Yeah."

"What do you mean by it being legal?"

"Well, I suppose you mean have I just proposed? I don't think I should do that until I've experienced these freaky or quirky encounters at various and sundry places that are strange but titillating?"

She opened her mouth to exclaim, as she grinned up at him. "You're really weird."

And with their exchange, Tweed felt now was the time to warn her. "You'd better adjust to the fact that one of these days, buttercup, you're going to have to sit down with the sheriff and tell him exactly what he wants to know. He is another man than he appears. He's a good lawman, and he is worried about what all happened out there in the hollow."

"I need to walk. I need to get away. I don't want—
I need—"

"Let's go swim."

"Yes."

She had no swimsuit. Although Tweed was willing
to skinny-dip, she declined doing that in the daylight.
They got Sam; then they went to the attic to hunt
through some trunks of things that had been Ethel's.
Sam went slowly through the clothes with sentimental
rememberings. He found a denim skirt, several shirts.
A jacket or two. And he found a one-piece woolen
swimsuit that had been mothproofed.

Connie hesitated about wearing Ethel's things, but
Sam said Ethel would have loaned them without
thinking twice about it.

Surprisingly, the suit fit Connie. It had boy-cuffed
legs and a very low back with narrow shoulder straps.
It was very attractive.

Tweed said so. He said, "If you have to wear
something, that's not bad."

"It's comfortable."

He groused, "Other women wear colored Band-
Aids."

She lifted her chin and mentioned, "Men wear long
shorts and are well covered—as they stand around
looking at the skimpy Band-Aids on the women."

"Wellll." He searched for a counterargument.
"Men are appreciative," he explained earnestly.
"When women parade around that way, men feel ob-
ligated to be courteous and—look."

"They're just being courteous?"

"Of course!" He was a little elaborate in his surprise. "You didn't realize that? Why else would men
be looking that way?"

"They're lechers."

He lifted protesting hands and shook his head. "No, no, no! Men are all raised by their mommas to be appreciators. They're taught to appreciate fine art, good food and Band-Aided women."

"Hah!"

# Ten

The lovers went to the pond. Tweed went in first, and Connie entered the water more timidly. She was a pool swimmer. They swam and played as she became used to pond swimming, and the ducks watched with some disdain at the humans' amateurish attempts to be ducks. The ducks were tolerant of the intrusion.

Of course, having been warned not to dive deeply, they had to explore the bottom. And it was cold. However, they had exercised enough by then that the cold was not only endurable but refreshing.

And swimming is freedom. Controlled danger. He was a good swimmer, and Connie was skilled. She was in command of the elements. It had been a chance happenstance that she be allowed that feeling at that particular time, and it gave her confidence.

They did eat an acceptable amount for lunch, and Jake didn't go into an attitude decline. Connie told

Jake, "You're a superb cook. You already know that, but I'm not a ranch hand. I'm a sedentary woman who will sit at a computer these next days, and I must eat discreetly or you will have to widen the doorways. *El comprehendo?*"

Anybody in Texas thinks he or she can throw in all sorts of Mexican-sounding words. And at times, they actually hit on something that's near enough. Jake did comprehend. He nodded quite seriously and went to his files.

But that night Connie slid out of Tweed's bed, hunted down her pills and took a sleeping pill. Tweed was aware, but he made no comment to Connie. However, the next day, he reported that to Sanford.

For almost a week, Connie put files into the computer. At one point she told Sam, "Another feed store would be more cost-effective."

Sam replied, "Well, Tyrone is an old friend."

"With that attitude," she said disapprovingly, "you'll never be a millionaire."

Sam was shocked, "Why would I want that much money?"

And she scoffed, "You're counterproductive."

Of course, the neighbors came to view the woman. Everyone knew about Connie and they wanted to see her for themselves. The women knew she'd snook-ered Tweed, and they were dying of curiosity. To all their surprise, they found Connie was a nice woman. She didn't fawn or snort or look down her nose. She was a lady. She behaved as one.

With that knowledge, they became her supporters. Everyone knew about the hollow and what had happened to her there. And the two roving men were monitored with more intense interest.

That was true of the men on Sam's place. They all felt possessive of Tweed's woman. They all knew she belonged to him, but she also belonged to Sam and the ranch, and she was there to share their loyalty.

They gave her a party. They had all the people around and about to come, and it was fun. But at the beginning, Dusty viewed the dress that hung on Connie like a potato sack, and he asked suspiciously, "Miss Connie, did Tweed pick out that dress?"

She smiled a tiny bit and replied, "Yes. He told me his taste is impeccable."

And Rusty replied, "Could he have said impossible instead of impeccable?"

Connie grinned and said, "Oh, maybe that's what he said." But she wore that dress.

The entire contingent at the ranch went on Connie's elegant diet until a revolt almost got out of hand. Then Jake slapped the men's usual fare on the table while he courteously served ambrosia to Connie.

She ate succulent and deliciously contrived nibbles. The men watched enviously. Finally Jake was convinced to give the men their hearty fare, but he had to make enough of Connie's tempting bits so that the men could have their share of those also.

Jake was put-upon. He sighed and sank down on a chair and sprawled in exhaustion and rolled his eyes and loved every compliment.

Sam told Connie, "You gotta know how much I appreciate you stretching Jake this-a way? He hasn't been challenged for a long time, and he's happier than I've ever seen him since we lost Ethel. I can hear him humming in the kitchen when he thinks everyone is gone.''

''A nuisance.'' She guessed that in sympathy.

Sam agreed with a solemn nod. ''People are so strange. If Ethel was still around, I wouldn't mind staying here and watching.''

The sheriff visited again and said, ''I think those two drifters are two of the three that abandoned Connie and her uncle to the other two. We think they're trying to find the hollow and have lost track of where it was. They expect to find the car still there. And the dope.

''We're leaving the panels empty—like somebody stole it. We've removed all traces of the fight. It looks like a peaceful place. The tools are back in the trunk and the hood's closed. We've made tracks to the road and a car's tires are apparent. If it rains, that'll be perfect. The place'd really look deserted. We've been promised rain again.''

Sam put in, ''Don't hold your breath.''

But it did rain. It rained just right. The mist, to begin with, opened all the tightly closed, water-preserving curls of vegetation. When they'd had a proper drink, the rain came down better. It drummed noisily on the roofs, and the animals frisked around with the unexpected surprise. Not the cats. They curled down into balls with their tails tucked around them, crouched in openings so they could watch the strangeness of rain.

It didn't thunder or carry on that way, it was just a good rain. A miracle. The ground was offended and tried to reject it, beading up the drops with dust and setting them aside. But eventually, the ground realized what was happening and allowed the water entrance.

The leaves and weeds and tree trunks and wood were washed, and the wet colors were simply eye pleasuring. The smell of the fresh air filled hungry lungs.

Tweed took Connie to test the hay in the far barn. "Have you ever made love in a hay pile?"

"No, I haven't." She was a little stiff.

"Well, yes, but how can I know you didn't let some guy fool around al-most that far in a barn on a rainy day?"

"Have you?"

"You're my first." He gave her a sweet smile.

"First? Who'll be your second?"

"Well, I do declare, you're the most suspicious woman I have *ever* met!"

He picked her up and tried to carry her up the mound of hay, but it was slithery and slippery, and they ended up laughing and tumbling. So they played, they burrowed, they slid down and they laughed.

Finally they lay back, still grinning and gasping for breath, and they held hands and looked at each other. He inquired of the languid beauty, "You know you're a miracle?"

And she replied seriously, "So are you."

"I love you with all my heart."

"Oh, Tweed, I don't feel whole enough to commit myself to such a pledge."

"Whole enough?"

"I'm not sure you aren't a harbor for me. You're protective and loving, and perhaps I just need you for that."

"And you suspect that you don't love me, you just need me?"

"I will have to be whole before I know." She was distressed.

"Well, without you, I'm only half of me."

"I don't mean to use you. I can't commit to you until I can know if that's what I'm doing. I feel so safe with you."

"That's not safety, that's being home in me, with me."

"Oh, Tweed. You are so wonderful."

"No, I'm only a man. But I'm one who loves you. I want more than that, but I won't trouble you until you're ready."

"How much more can I give you?"

"Besides love? Well, let's see now. There's living together and being married and having kids and quarreling and making up and hassling each other and taking up for each other and being on each other's side and telling our feelings and discussing the gossip and going places together and—"

"You mean that, after some years and having several kids, we'll finally get to see other people?"

"Well, you might not realize right away that I've isolated you so much, not right at first. It would take a while, I'm so fascinating and all. And there'd be all the ways I want to try it in different places and things like that."

"Like being in a barn on a rainy day, on a pile of slippery straw?"

"Hay."

"Hey, yourself."

"No, I wasn't calling your attention to me. You called this straw. This is hay."

"Oh." And she laughed out loud.

"You are a darling." He turned over on his side and raised up to lean on one elbow. His eye crinkles were deepened, and he gazed on her in pleasure.

"You're making your move."

A tad disgruntled, he chided her. "You're not supposed to mention that you realize that. You're supposed to be aware but in a casual manner. You're supposed to lick your lips to call my attention to them. Then you shift your shoulders so your sweet breasts rise up and ask for my regard. And you move your knees so that I know they're there."

"How did you know all that? Who taught you that?"

"You do it in bed."

"Really? I wasn't aware of doing that." She licked her lips thoughtfully; then her eyes widened and she rubbed her lips with the thumb side of her hand. "I didn't mean that!"

"Yes, you did, too. You do all sorts of things to call my attention to you."

"What?"

"You breathe. You move. You walk. You lie in my bed and you sigh. You turn your head and your eyes look at me in such a sultry way."

"You have a vivid imagination. You make it sound as if I do those things deliberately."

He was offended. "It isn't deliberate? You don't try to lure me?"

"Well, I do let you touch me."

"You don't want me to?"

"Well. Yes."

"So if I do... that... you don't mind?"

"That's shocking."

He moved his hand erotically. "I've done that to you before."

"You always did the preliminaries first."

"What... preliminaries?"

"You said nice things and kissed me and petted me a little on my back and stomach before you did that."

"But you knew what I was aiming for, didn't you?"

"Yes, but—"

"So why can't you be as triggered as I am?"

"I guess my mind doesn't work the way yours does."

He was appalled. "You don't think about sex the entire time?"

"No."

He slowly lay back on the hay as if he'd fainted in dismay.

She leaned up over him. "I didn't mean to discourage you."

So with her move and concern, he took up on that immediately. "Of course," he said rather faintly, "I am discouraged."

Earnestly concerned, she told him, "I really like the way you do... those things... to me."

"You never touch me."

"I have, too!" She protested. "Just this morning I... And last night you were shocked and exclaimed!"

"I was whispering."

"You can exclaim very scandalized in a whisper."

He admitted, "I just didn't want Sam to realize he's harboring a scarlet woman."

"See? I *do* do those things."

"Show me."

She didn't know quite where to begin. She hesitated, her lips parted, her eyes busy looking at various parts of him. She did stare. She said, "You're so obvious." And she had a tough time getting the zipper to work. He gasped once and he jerked a couple of times and he said, "Be careful," very seriously.

"Did I hurt you?"

"You're about to set me off."

But even under that threat, she did persevere, and she was successful, in every way one can be under those circumstances.

It wasn't until the second time and after a nap that he said he would allow her to roll on the condom.

They were both naked, lying on their clothes. She was tousled and some parts of her body had become reddened by his attentions. Her hair was mussed and had straw in it. He smiled at her. "You can roll it on."

"You can do that." She was blushing.

"What if I broke both my arms and the twins are only six months old?"

"Twins?" she inquired carefully.

"There're just times like that, buttercup, when a woman needs to know how to roll on a condom. You need to practice. You have a lot to learn, and we need to take advantage of every opportunity... if you can really love me."

"I believe I do."

"We need to be sure. I'm sunk already. If we go on this-a way all the time, and you decide you're not serious about me, just think what that would do to me." He was on a roll. "You have to consider that I'm a human person, and I had a heart, up until now. If you should ever leave me, I'd probably die or I'd be like Sam and just wait around for it."

"I'm not toying with you."

He raised up his head and looked down him at her hand.

"I mean that—well, I'm . . ."

"What?" he encouraged.

"I think..." She looked around the barn in some distress.

He became a little uneasy that he'd pushed the teasing too far.

She took a deep breath and looked at him. "I need to go to the hollow and look at it. I need to remember. I need to exorcise that place from my nightmares."

He was appalled.

She was agitated. "Uh. Tweed. Will you go with me?"

"Yes." He was stunned. What had he done with his teasing and tempting?

"You would probably respect me more if I went by myself."

"No."

"It's raining."

"Yeah."

"We probably couldn't go until it clears."

"No." What was he to do? What would he do if she got out there and flipped back into the coma? He had to call Sanford. The sheriff! That's who he needed.

So Tweed was somewhat distracted as she rolled on the condom. The distraction probably saved him from an untoward ejaculation. But she did get his attention, and his lovemaking was so compassionate and tender that she got teary eyed.

"Oh, Tweed," she said in a watery voice. "There is no man like you in all the world."

"Yeah. I love you, Connie."

Later that day, Tweed loaded an extra pistol and set up a target in the barn. After that, they practiced hitting specific things. Tweed would call the shots. "The window!" Then, "The ladder!" And "The door!" "In back of you. The tree limb outside."

He was somewhat soothed that she could really shoot, but all the guys on the place gathered at a safe distance and yelled to know what the hell was going on?

Connie laughed and explained that Tweed was entertaining her on a rainy day.

That made the men slide unbelieving looks at Tweed. Any man knows what to do with a woman on a rainy day, and target shooting wasn't one of them. However, they did see the haystack had been disheveled, so maybe Tweed wasn't as stupid as they thought?

Finding a way to use the phone without Connie around wasn't easy. She worked on the computer and argued with Sam and got their office efficient.

Then she began to teach Tweed how to use the computer. He was exquisitely reluctant. Curious to try but awkward to expose himself as ignorant where she was expert. He took to the computer like the ducks to the pond.

He had Sam take Connie down to the hangar to get a listing of supplies and parts. That took them all of one day. While they were gone, Tweed talked to everyone in the county. He told them all about what he planned to do.

The area around the hollow was under surveillance, by any and all of the surrounding inhabitants, who were very aware as to why Tweed asked that they be particularly alert at that time. None told Tweed that the sheriff had radioed them all, with the alert in code.

The sheriff had done that right after Tweed first informed him of the projected visit.

And the listeners knew that the purpose of the visit was to try to trigger Connie's reluctant memory.

The night before they went to the hollow, Connie took a sleeping pill and slept the drugged sleep of oblivion. Tweed was wakeful.

They got up the next morning, and the sheriff was at the breakfast table. He gave Tweed a steady look and said, "I know the questions we need answered. I know what to do."

Connie hesitated just a tad; then she sat down, but she did nod her head at the sheriff.

He said, "I admire what you're doing. It'll help you, but it could help us. Say out loud everything that comes to your mind. What you see. Listen and tell me their words. Names. Anything. Any habits the guys show. Pulling on a ear. Scratching. Anything."

She shivered.

Tweed was appalled. He didn't know what to do.

She said, "It's cooler today. I'll need a jacket."

It was October. It was lovely outside. Cool. Pleasant. Everything looked as it should at that time of the year. There were flamboyant trees, but the colors were subtle. Even the dead grasses were beautiful in their dying shades. It was a seasonal cycle, a natural death, not just lack of rain.

At the last minute, Dusty decided to go along. He argued if they were to monitor the hollow, he ought to know everything. So there were six people in the plane. Tweed wasn't the pilot. The plane carried three motorbikes lashed inside.

They had flown over the hollow to look around. They didn't want to surprise anyone. They weren't laying a trap, they were trying to get Connie to remember more. They landed beyond the hollow.

The track ran alongside the flatland where the plane came down. The two men with them stayed with the plane. They were outside on the ground and alert.

The sheriff used one motorbike, Dusty the other, and Tweed carried Connie on the third one. They eased along, going gingerly over the difficult way and down into the hollow. They went carefully off the primitive track until they came to the place.

The men were excessively alert. Connie was very quiet. They shut off the motors and hid the keys. They stood in the silence, listening.

The sheriff had warned Tweed and Dusty not to comment at all. They were there for Connie. But if she talked, he wanted to guide her thinking, her remembrance.

She walked around. She stopped dead when she saw the car still there. She stared at it.

The sheriff said, "You're remembering. Tell me."

"We came down that track. I was driving. It was obvious I'd missed a turn. I couldn't get out the other side, and we had to turn around to go back. There was no place to turn, and I backed onto that rock. We were stuck.

"We tried to rock it off, and we couldn't. We really tried. We had water and some food with us. Uncle Clyde had been out here and knew to have water and food along. And he had the signal tire and flammable oil. We didn't set that until we had to face the fact we would need help. We lit the fire the first thing the next morning."

"Were you concerned at that time?"

"Not really."

"What happened?"

"It wasn't long before that car came. There were five men in it." Connie stared at the ground and was silent.

After too long, Tweed said, "Connie?"

She looked up as if she was underwater. But she began to talk. It was as if she was hypnotized. She stared unseeing at Tweed and described exactly what happened in those next days. She told of the abuse of her, the beating of her uncle that she'd tried to prevent. And his body being thrown aside.

She talked by rote. Her memory unwound as if it was an old film running in her head. She told descriptions as if she looked at the faces in describing them. She put names with the faces. First names. Nicknames. She told what they did to her. They would allow her no clothing. She told how the other three men took the Moody car and left, and what had happened after that—her uncle miraculously reviving and getting the rifle.

The sheriff validated it. "So it was him?"

"Yes. But he did only that. He killed them."

Then she said with great sadness, "He had no last word for me. He was dead before he hit the ground. I put his body into the car. There were prowling coyotes. Scavenger birds."

The sheriff clarified, "And the two were dead?"

She confirmed it, "Carrion." She would have left them in the open.

Tweed felt a shiver at her word, it was so coldly said.

The sheriff asked, "And that night?"

"I had the rifle."

He pressed, "The others were to come back?"

"Yes." Then she looked at Tweed and focused. "When the plane landed..." She gulped. "It was a man. It was help. I don't remember much else."

"You've been a real help to us." Then the sheriff talked into a button. "Did you get all that?"

An empathetic male voice said softly, "Yeah."

The sheriff said, "I'm going up on top. Dusty, come along. It might be a good idea for us to look around. See if you remember anything else. But, Connie, this isn't a place of horror. The horrors are gone. This is just a wooded place where something terrible happened. It was the creatures who came here, it wasn't the place that harmed you."

She said quietly, "Thank you."

The sheriff and Dusty left.

Tweed was beside himself in agitation for her. He appeared calm, but he was not. His emotions were high and he was in tight control. He asked, "Do you want to look around?"

"Perhaps on the other side of the road? This is a very isolated place."

"Yes."

The birds began to inquire of one another just what was happening in their place? There was an occasional rustle in the underbush. Connie jumped and gasped.

Tweed said, "Lizard."

"I'm a little spooked."

"You are magnificent."

"How can you say that?"

"You survived."

"My uncle—"

"And you fought for him. He saved your life."

"They were never going to kill me. They planned to *sell* me in Central America."

"They probably would have made more off you than the dope they had in the panels of the car."

"They had dope hidden?" She hadn't known.

"It was taken out. The car's empty. It's wired. If anyone touches it, the whole county will know."

"I like the way the people have rallied around."

"They do that all the time, with everything. They're a nuisance most of the time, but in a crisis, you can't beat having them rally 'round."

"Tweed, no one can beat you. You are wonderful. I love you so very much. Can you still love me? Can you love me after all this happened?"

"I've known what happened all along. It happened to you. You are the same as you've always been. You're perfect. Being here and enduring all that had nothing to do with you except to prove that you are a remarkable woman."

"I went into shock."

"Only an insensitive person could go through what you went through and not need some time to adjust."

"Do you really think all that or are you prejudiced?"

"I do love you. More now than before. It'll probably be like that all the rest of our lives. My love will grow. But even if all this had happened to another woman, I couldn't help but admire her for surviving."

"I wouldn't have without Uncle Clyde."

"You would have found a way. Here or wherever you were taken."

She looked around the hollow, and her head lifted. Her back straightened. "I am strong. I'd forgotten that for a while."

"You never did forget. You just were healing from a terrible time."

She looked at Tweed. "I love you."

"That does make it easier for you to put up with me. You got your work cut out for you, do you know that?" He took her arm, and they walked along the rutted, rocky track to the top of the rim to look down onto the hollow.

"It's peaceful." She turned her head, seeing.

"The animals and birds are being patient, waiting for us to leave."

Unbeknownst to them, Dusty had returned for his motorbike. Standing unobserved, he listened.

Connie said, "It's strange, but seeing the hollow as just a place has helped me."

Tweed replied gently, "I'm glad. I hated to have you come here. When you said this would be the way to clear yourself, I was upset. I called the sheriff and as—"

"You called him?"

"I didn't know if I should let you do it."

"I came here, Tweed Brown, because I wanted you to know that I'm not a ninny!"

"A...ninny?"

"A thumb-sucking coward."

"I swear to you that I never, for one minute, including the time you were flat-out in the hospital, never did I think you were a coward."

"Do you mean I went through all this for nothing?"

"You went through it so's you'd know you were whole and could love me properly."

"I've been loving you improperly?"

"No. You've used restraint."

"That's . . . restraint?"

"Yeah. It'll be interesting to see how you act when you're loving full out."

She looked at him for a long time before she said, "How could I have been so lucky as to have you find me." It wasn't a question. Her face was soft and her eyes were gentle.

He was so moved. He almost spoke a couple of times before he said, "I think it's time for Salty and Felicia to come down and meet you. I suppose you'll have your contingency back to check me out?"

Mildly, she looked off to the horizon and mentioned, "I wonder where Gregory is by now?"

And Tweed laughed as his hand enclosed hers.

She said quite sadly, "Actually, I have no people."

"Who were all those kinfolk roosting in the waiting room, hovering?"

"No parents. No siblings." Her voice was rather pensive.

"Well, you already know that I don't have any, either. Not any kith nor kin. We'll start fresh."

Dusty heard it all.

The surviving three men who had been responsible for the capture of Connie and the resulting murder of her uncle in that hollow were never apprehended, nor was the Moody car recovered.

There was a rumor the third man had been sighted near the two under surveillance. But that was never confirmed.

Not long after that, the two suspicious men in the area vanished. No sign of them was ever found. The possibility that they could have slipped away through the watched area was puzzling.

Sam's crew from the Fuller ranch listened politely to the speculation about a helicopter rescue. There were others who scoffed and said any whirlybird would have had one hell of a time escaping notice, much less those who might have rescued the two under the area's microscope.

Sam's men expressed agreeing surprise over that. They speculated about the seep in the hollow which they'd discovered accidentally was very dangerous quicksand. They wondered if the three might have blundered into that?

There were scoffing responses.

While others in the area kept chewing on where those three were and what could have happened to them, Sam's men didn't appear concerned that the three would ever surface again.

The Fuller men were the only ones who lost interest, and it was curious that the others' speculation about the fate of the three rather bored them.

Salty and Felicia came to visit at the Fuller ranch, and like all good actors, they fit in perfectly. Susanne and Cray came over from San Antonio. Mike and Sara visited from the army post where he was stationed. Even Tom turned up.

Then Tweed and Connie went to Temple, Ohio, for Christmas at the Browns'. There Connie met most of the rest of the family. And Tweed saw that his foster sister, Carol, and her policeman were well suited. That

they were suited tugged briefly at Tweed's heart in an
echo of his youthful infatuation.

It was in April that Tweed and Connie were married in TEXAS at the ranch. An amazing number of
Browns were added to the staggering area guests, and
it was a Frolic. The fiddles! The dancing! The beer.
The flirtations.

The TEXAS weather was perfect, naturally, and
tents were rented and raised to hold the overflow of
guests. The Brown offsprings' offspring found that
especially delightful.

With Jake in dramatic command, the food made the
tables groan before the overstuffed people also
groaned.

And there was laughter.

Tweed looked on his love with such tender eyes.
And he knew the miracle that had started so horribly
with a burning-tire signal had turned into a blessing.

Who can figure out the patterns of lives?

Connie asked her love, "Do you think we knew
each other before this time?"

Tweed smiled on his love and replied, "I wouldn't
be surprised."

Their lives were good, and their interests ex-
panded. Tweed became very active as a good citizen
whose attention to the area became possessive. That
tossed-away child had finally found a home.

Connie figured his attention to the ways and poli-
tics of the area was because of the children he gathered even before they had any of their own.

But it wasn't Salty who found the new kids for Tweed and Connie to raise. It was a revitalized and interested and involved Sam.

*     *     *     *     *

# Take 4 bestselling love stories FREE

## Plus get a FREE surprise gift!

## Special Limited-time Offer

**Mail to Silhouette Reader Service™**

P.O. Box 609
Fort Erie, Ontario
L2A 5X3

**YES!** Please send me 4 free Silhouette Desire® novels and my free surprise gift. Then send me 6 brand-new novels every month, which I will receive months before they appear in bookstores. Bill me at the low price of $2.49 each plus 25¢ delivery and GST*. That's the complete price and—compared to the cover prices of $2.99 each—quite a bargain! I understand that accepting the books and gift places me under no obligation ever to buy any books. I can always return a shipment and cancel at any time. Even if I never buy another book from Silhouette, the 4 free books and the surprise gift are mine to keep forever.

326 BPA AJJ3

| | |
|---|---|
| Name | (PLEASE PRINT) |
| Address | Apt. No. |
| City | Province  Postal Code |

This offer is limited to one order per household and not valid to present Silhouette Desire® subscribers.
*Terms and prices are subject to change without notice.
Canadian residents will be charged applicable provincial taxes and GST.

CDES-93RR                                    ©1990 Harlequin Enterprises Limited

**by Ann Major**

Take a walk on the wild side with Ann Major's sizzling
stories featuring Honey, Midnight...and Innocence!

*IN SEPTEMBER, YOU EXPERIENCED...*

**WILD HONEY** Man of the Month
A clash of wills set the stage for an electrifying romance for
J. K. Cameron and Honey Wyatt.

*NOW ENJOY...*

**WILD MIDNIGHT** November 1993
Heat Up Your Winter
A bittersweet reunion turns into a once-in-a-lifetime adventure for
Lacy Douglas and Johnny Midnight.

*AND IN FEBRUARY 1994, LOOK FOR...*

**WILD INNOCENCE** Man of the Month
One man's return sets off a startling chain of events for
Innocence Lescuer and Raven Wyatt.

Let your wilder side take over with this exciting series—only from
Silhouette Desire!

---

# SILHOUETTE® *Desire*®

## HAS THE WINTER
## WEATHER GOT YOU DOWN?
## IS THE TEMPERATURE
## JUST TOO COLD? THEN

HEAT UP *your* WINTER

## COMING IN NOVEMBER
## ONLY FROM SILHOUETTE DESIRE

Silhouette Desire's most sensuous writers bring you six sexy stories—and six stunning heroes—guaranteed to get your temperature rising.

### Look for

| #817 | TWEED by Lass Small |
| #818 | NOT JUST ANOTHER PERFECT WIFE by Robin Elliott · |
| #819 | WILD MIDNIGHT by Ann Major |
| #820 | KEEGAN'S HUNT by Dixie Browning |
| #821 | THE BEST REVENGE by Barbara Boswell |
| #822 | DANCLER'S WOMAN by Mary Lynn Baxter |

When it comes to sinfully seductive heroes and provocative love stories...no one does it better than Silhouette Desire!

SDWH

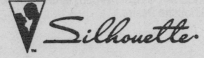